Testimonials

"SISTERLY is one of those thrillers that keeps you guessing with each turn of the page. The characters are unique, developed and will surprise you. Loved it!" - Armand Rosamilia, author of the crime thriller *Dirty Deeds* series

"Sisterly is a wonderful, haunting tale, a great concept, and Jorja wrote it with perfect execution. She describes her scenes and people so vividly I saw them in my mind's eye as though I was watching a movie. Which this book should become one. It pulls you into another dimension. Slowly I was right there in the middle, being swallowed by the paranormal? Superstitions? Like a detective, I kept going, trying to figure it out. Where was Ms. Jorja taking me? The more I guessed with each page the more I was wrong, and I giggled in delight. I told myself, *she has me now!* I can tell you it wasn't predictable! She moves you through time and places, but you know not all is well, like the character in the story, you become a part of it all and start to feel like you are going insane along with her! With each page, my heartbeat quickened, and as I got closer to the end... BOOM! Out of nowhere, she hits you with a riveting dose of reality... I got the chills reading the last four pages of this story. What is one's reality? What power does our inner psyche hold? What reality can we manifest when we are faced with a tragedy mixed with old folklore? Hold on to your brain matter while reading this story, because it will Blow. Your. Mind!"- Robin H. Soprano, Author of *A SOULMATE'S PROMISE* and *ABSINTHE*

J.D Oliva

Sisterly

Sisterly

Two sisters, one love.

Confined to one town.

One mistake

and one house...

J. D. Oliva

J.D Oliva

Sisterly by J. D. Oliva
Copyright © 2017 by Jorja DuPont Oliva
Copy Edit by Karin Nicely
Cover Photo by Rowen S. Poole
Cover Layout by Alexandra King
Interior Layout and Pagination by Jorja DuPont Oliva
Sisterly by Jorja DuPont Oliva
338p. ill. cm.
ISBN (softcover) 9780999183809
Library of Congress Control Number: 2017910880

All Rights Reserved. No part of this book may be reproduced, stored in a retrieval system, or transmitted in any form or by any means, electronic, mechanical, photocopying, recording, or otherwise, without permission in writing from JD & RB Enterprises Inc. Publishing.

JD & RB Enterprises Inc.
PO Box 1774
Bunnell, FL 32110
jorjao@msn.com
www.jorjao2013.com

Printed in the United States of America

J.D Oliva

This book is dedicated to my sisters:

Tressie Paytas

and

Trudy Tedder

I know we have our differences, but we also share our sameness.

With a deep appreciation to both of you, *Sisterly* is proof I am the craziest sister now!

J.D Oliva

Sisterly

*Sisterly bonds start before birth,
never to be broken,
nor to die in the afterlife.*
- Jorja DuPont Oliva

*A sister is a gift to the heart,
a friend to the spirit,
a golden thread to the meaning of life.*
-Isadora James

*Sweet is the voice of a sister
in the season of sorrow.*
-Benjamin Disraeli

A ministering angel shall my sister be.
-William Shakespeare

J.D Oliva

ACKNOWLEDGMENTS
Thanks to You All!

Rachael Miller - for being my first proofreader and my friend. You helped me lead *Sisterly* in the direction she needed to be. **Rhonda Bracewell** - as always, your support never needs to be overlooked. **Bobby Kretzman** - for encouraging me and giving me great ideas for *Sisterly*. **Michael Ray King** - you have taught me so many things, my appreciation for you is far beyond what words can express. I shall call you my mentor. **Karin Nicely** - you were a pleasure to work with on my edits and a beautiful model for my front cover. Sometimes everything we need is right in front of us and it takes an editor to help us find it. **Rowen S. Poole**, photographer- for creating a wonderful picture for my cover. **Chris Balsam** – you, my friend, are a true friend, and thank you for encouraging me to write. **Armanda Rosamillia** - your time to read my story and your encouragements are priceless. You inspire me! **Robin H. Soprano** - I always love bouncing ideas with you. Your creative energy keeps my head on straight and inspires me. **Cilla Williams** and **Annie Hizine** - for being you. Strong black women should not go without being noticed. You are admired, and you have given me strength as a woman. **Jenn Raymond** - each new day is a fresh start to a new tomorrow. You have inspired me with your determination. **Laurie Cuccurullo** – for late-night chats on writing and for PJ night. **Dominic, Nicholas,** and **Zachary** - thanks for understanding my passion. Finally yet importantly, I am always thankful for my **family, friends,** and **fans!**

J.D Oliva

FOREWORD

Who motivates the author? What energy causes one author to blossom and another to wilt? Ultimately, how do writers grow their craft?

In 2013, Jorja DuPont Oliva enrolled in my "How to Write Your Book in 30 Days!" workshop mainly as support for her mother, who desired to write a book and also enrolled. Jorja's personality was somewhat opposite to her mother's. Jorja was quiet and shy, and Linda loved to talk! I could not have imagined that Jorja would rise up to answer those questions in the previous paragraph for me.

These days, I refer to Jorja as an "author's author." Here's what I mean by that statement: Jorja's first book, *Chasing Butterflies in the Magical Garden*, cradled a wonderful story in basically a fifty-thousand-word paragraph. Despite its unorthodox presentation, I read the manuscript. I felt the story play out within me. I then wondered if Jorja would be up to the task of rewrite and edit.

Not only did Jorja work hard during the editing process – she learned. The first draft of her second book, *Chasing Butterflies in the Mystical Forest*, came to life dramatically more pristine and organized. Along with utilizing her understanding of the structure of a book and how it should look, she employed many of the lessons from the edits of her first novel.

Then came the third book, *Chasing Butterflies in the Unseen Universe*, where she played interesting authorial games with timelines and the future. Jorja describes these books as magical realism. This quiet, shy writer completed a trilogy in less than three years, but she did not stop there.

Jorja also wrote and published short stories. She wrote a play – Yes! A play! – then took on crafting a screenplay for her trilogy. Now she has not only completed her fourth book, *Sisterly*, but she's also learning the ropes of publishing.

As a motivational speaker, I've been asked many times, "Who motivates the motivator?" The answer I most identify with also applies to those of us who write or create, which is this: Motivation comes and goes. Drive wins the day.

When we're driven, as Jorja most certainly demonstrates, good things happen. I've seen her motivation lag. All the writers I know suffer from this malady. Yet Jorja's drive keeps her moving forward. She's driven to challenge herself and to improve.

Sisterly stands as her next step. Jorja delves more into the psychological and paranormal in this book. She challenges the reader to be sharp, to pay attention. She engages. She weaves us a memorable tale.

After she completed her trilogy, I wondered if she would struggle to break out of the confines of that three-book world and into something different. I should never have questioned. *Sisterly* has made a believer out of me in Jorja's quest to forge ahead as an author – ever growing, ever challenging herself, ever delivering for her readers.

Sisterly

With Jorja's example, I can now define "author" as someone driven to express their creativity in writing. Who motivates the author? Jorja motivates me, but who really cares? The answer to project completion stands as drive – that intangible inner motor and focus we gain when we chase our dreams. The energy of that internal drive is modeled for me in this book. Ultimately, the exquisite growth of an author flows out of an inner voice, driven by an inner desire to create, and is exemplified by the end products.

Sisterly comes as another step into a budding future for Jorja. We as readers win because Jorja as an author continues to learn and grow. Allow her characters to whisk you off into their world. Slide into Jorja's imagination to find the escape her fiction affords us. Be thankful for driven authors, especially an author's author.

Michael Ray King

"Go Write and You Won't Go Wrong – How to Write Your Book in 30 Days!"

Five-time Royal Palm Literary Award winning author

Palm Coast, FL

J.D Oliva

Prologue

"Who are you?" Dr. Chang asked me as she opened her notebook just as she had always done during my session with her. She always started with the same questions.

"I am Janie Edwards," I said as if she did not know who I was.

"Why are you here, Janie Edwards?" Dr. Chang jotted down some notes and looked up from her note pad. "It's been a long time since you have come to see me."

I was sure glad she remembered me, finally. "I am here because I just received word from an attorney that my son, the son I put up for adoption, wants to find his *family." I did not tell her the whole story.*

"I see..." Dr. Chang wrote more in her tablet. "Please tell me more."

She knew I was not much for opening up about my personal life, but I was there to get answers. "I left my hometown because I was pregnant. No one in my family knew; just me."

"And the father?" Dr. Chang asked.

"No, I never told anyone," I told her, but there was more that needed to be said.

"Was the father's name on the birth certificate, the original one? The papers filled out by the hospital, before the adoption paperwork?" Dr. Chang peeked over

her glasses, waiting for a response from me.

"Yes," I answered. I wasn't so sure I wanted to explain the whole story, but I did because I needed to get it all off my chest. I needed to figure it all out. "But... the father, Dillon McCrane, is now married to my sister, Brea."

"I see, and you are worried this son's lawyer is going to contact them as well?" Dr. Chang asked.

"Yes, and I'm worried for Brea. This could really destroy her. They have kids of their own now." My face crumbled into my hands only to get a grip on my thoughts. "You see, I hated that place, despised it, and now... I have to get back to Brea and Dillon before they find out." I looked at

Dr. Chang. "I would rather they hear it from me first — you know?"

"So why are you here, Janie Edwards?" Dr. Chang asked me again. That moment, I realized exactly what I needed to do.

Chapter 1

"Empty" blinked on the dashboard. Janie Edwards' rusty, blue 1980 Datsun 210 hatchback chugged its way into the filling station just north of town. The town she had grown up in. The town she had never felt she belonged in.

Now at the age of fifty, it seemed as though her feelings were more than just intuition. Her soul was telling her what her life had planned for her: constant hardship. And this town was the start of it all.

She believed reason always guided her to where she needed to be. At least that was what the signs had always lead her to believe, and thanks to her visit with Dr. Chang, today she had a good reason. The only man she'd ever loved lived in this town, and he had married her sister, Brea. It was time to tell him why she had left — and goodbye. Closure, forgiveness, and peace of mind. But more than anything, making amends with her sister called for her to return.

Thirty years had passed since she'd stepped foot on Florida soil. *Born to this soil and die upon this soil.* At least that was how she believed her family felt. She had not had any contact with any relatives since the day she'd left.

"Sunshine state," Janie huffed as the car rolled to a slow stall that hopefully would not be noticed. The Florida sun beamed onto the car. Waves of heat escaped the asphalt like souls from the gates of hell. Luckily, she only had to push the car three feet to the gas pump.

Janie pushed in the clutch and rattled the five-speed into neutral. She climbed over the stick-shift into the passenger seat, opened the car door to the passenger side, and stepped out. She hated the fact she had to get out of her own car that way, but it was the only way out. Only a fractional amount of time had passed since a car had sideswiped her. With the resulting broken pelvis and many other broken bones, she'd spent who knows how much time in the hospital. Janie still struggled with knowing exactly how long it had been.

"She'll be lucky if she lives," doctors had babbled as they frantically worked to save her. By some unknown force, the car had made it out with only a huge dent in the driver's-side door, which made the door unable to open. So the car had still been drivable, but after getting back on the road, the AC and heat had gone on the fritz.

Janie reached her hand in through the open window, grabbed her pack of smokes, pulled one out, and lit it. She took a big draw; she deserved it, didn't she? Janie made her way to the back of the car and pushed it up to the gas pump as the cigarette dangled from her lip.

"Can't be smoking by the pumps, ma'am," a young Southern male voice startled her. He stood wearing a mechanic's blue jumpsuit. Janie tossed the cigarette to the ground and stepped it out. "Dangerous," he said as he approached her. "Must've ran out of gas, huh?"

Damn righteous, nosey, little town. She hurried to the passenger-side window, reached in, and pulled up the emergency brake to stop the car from drifting. "That's right! Out of gas," she groaned as she wiped her hands on her faded Levi's. *Some things never change.*

Exhaling, placing her hands on her hips, Janie turned to face the young fellow. "This is a gas station, isn't it?" Her sarcasm was obvious. "Do the Dandys still own this place?" she asked the young man as she wiped flakes of crumbs from her black tank top, remnants from her quick stop at the fast-food joint at the interstate exit. She smiled when she noticed the crook in his nose. One of the traits all the Dandy boys carried, besides the big bulgy, blue eyes. He had both.

"I'm a Russell. My grandpa is a Dandy. My momma's daddy. My Uncle John owns the place now. Hi, I'm Andy." Andy placed his hand out as an introduction.

"Probably a good thing you aren't a Dandy or you would have been Andy Dandy." Janie laughed and shook his hand. "I couldn't resist." She smiled as she moved her hands back to her hips. Her sarcasm always showed itself when she felt like someone was trying to keep her on the straight and narrow. Alternatively, point out the obvious.

You owe it to yourself to figure it all out. She reminded herself of what he had told her the day she'd left town thirty years ago. It had become her life motto. *Hell, so far it ain't pointing me to no life of righteousness, that's for sure.* Maybe, coming back to this place, she could figure it all out.

"You want it filled up?" he asked as he unscrewed the gas cap.

"Just put ten in for now." She had all but forgotten about full-service gas stations. They were obsolete in this day and time. Of course, this town was always two steps behind the rest of the world.

"Is the Cramers' old hotel still in business?" she asked,

knowing her sleeping arrangements were not going to be with family. She was the black sheep, and no one accepted her unruly behavior. Nor did she want to hear about everything the rest of the kin had accomplished.

"No, ma'am. They tore that building down a few years back. A bunch of squatters took up residence there. The town's people voted to get rid of the riff-raff." Andy stopped the gas pump at ten dollars and recapped the tank. He wiped his hands on a greasy garage rag that hung from his pocket.

Janie's grin flat lined when the memory of her squatting days returned. Living on the streets. The righteous always considered people in those situations as being riff-raff. She was a good person, only down on her luck — well, most of the time. Sure, she'd done things she was not proud of, but she'd done them to survive. With many of the squatters, that was also the case. The ones who brought themselves back... now, they were not even close to being riff-raff.

"Is there any places around this town I could possibly rent a room?"

"Sure, off of Moody Street by the tracks. There is an old yella house, been renovated. Old colored woman owns the place." Andy's bulgy blue eyes batted at the sun beaming down. "She rents out rooms. Not a lot of people stay there, though. They say she's a bit strange; as for me, I think the old woman is a saint." Andy wipes his sweat from his brow. "Ms. Francis."

"Sounds like my kind of place." Janie smiled as she handed him a ten-dollar bill. His hand remained in front of her, obviously waiting for more money to follow. "Oh." Janie dug in her pockets, pulled out a dollar-fifty in quarters, and slapped it on top of the ten-dollar bill. "Sorry about that. Hope you don't mind change."

"Might get me a pop from the soda machine over yonder. Appreciate it." Andy nodded and returned into the station, its every available space seemingly packed full of hubcaps and lines of oil containers. Janie inhaled and released before taking her next step back to her car. She stopped again at the passenger door, preparing to climb over the seat to the driver's side. She shook her head, got in, and wriggled her way across the seat.

Chapter 2

Janie's car coasted to the stop sign by the tracks. She stared at the old yellow house. It seemed harmless, looked well taken care of. The windows were dark, but maybe it was to keep the hot Florida sun from warming the house. *Hey, just being energy efficient,* she thought. The back of the house connected to an old eight-foot wooden privacy fence that surrounded a good amount of property. Several coats of paint peeled from the fence's surface. A Virginia creeper crawled its way from the other side, peeking out, watching her arrive. *Maybe there's a pool behind that fence.* Well, whatever *was* back there was definitely private.

The old yellow house was embraced by a porch that wrapped all the way around, stopping just short of the fencing. Cats of all colors lazily lingered on railings and steps as the sun spotlighted through the clouds. Each cat's tail waved, motioning like a little finger to come join him or her. Janie pulled her car into the gravel driveway. With her hands still gripping the steering wheel, she stared up at the second-story window. There stood someone watching her through a parted curtain, almost knowingly expecting her.

"It's better than going home," Janie sighed in surrender and turned the ignition to the off position. She inhaled and blew slowly out through her puckered lips. Dread danced around her head, but she knew she had to face this place, this town.

She crawled over the stick-shift, opened the passenger door, and backed her way out of the car.

"What you need?" a voice snapped from behind her. Janie quickly turned to see an old colored woman standing with arms perched on her hips. The woman's eyebrows narrowed, wrinkling her nose and making the whites of her eyes seem almost scary. *No wonder people think she is strange.*

"Hi, I'm Janie. Ms. Francis, is it?" She stretched her hand out to be polite. "I heard you rent rooms, and I need a place to stay."

"I don't rent nothin'." Ignoring Janie's hand, Ms. Francis spit. "You needs a place to sleep, you works for it here. I don't take no money from strangers; only the fruits of labor works here," Ms. Francis said as she smoothed her white apron stained with what appeared to be something of a brownish-red color.

"Work? What kind of work?" Janie scanned the property to see what she could possibly do to earn her a place to sleep.

"How long you plan on stayin'?" Ms. Francis spit again, but this time she turned partially away.

"A few days, a week at the most," Janie answered. The heat of facing her family warmed its way up her spine, and sweat began to moisten her neck, making her long brown hair cling to it. She gathered up her hair, spun it around her finger, and then rolled it into a bun. "Excuse me a second." She reached into the car to grab a bobby pin from the ashtray. That was where she kept her change and small trinkets. She shoved the pin through the bun to secure it and then grabbed her pack of cigarettes. "Do you mind if I have a smoke?" She waved the pack of Camels, surrendering.

"Nope, you do what you gots ta do." Ms. Francis nods. "I gots lots of guests I needs help with. Cleaning their rooms and changing their sheets. Then I gots to make sure they eats something."

Janie glanced around, noticing that no one was within sight but the lazy felines that lay on the porch. *This is probably why they think she is strange.* She imagines having guests. *This should be the easiest job I have ever had. She is old. Probably senile.*

She pulled a cigarette from the pack and lit it. She took a drag and, looking around, exhaled the smoke. "I can do this. I actually worked in Texas at a Holiday Inn Express a few years back."

"This ain't no fancy hotel, youngin'. Just a big house full of guests." Ms. Francis leaned in to whisper, "Ornery ones, too."

Janie stretched her hand out again, hoping this go round Ms. Francis would actually shake it. "You have a deal, Ms. Francis." The snarling look Ms. Francis had carried suddenly changed to a jolly grin with teeth as pretty and white as marshmallows. Janie smiled back as she shook hands with her new boss.

Janie took another drag then ground out the cigarette with her heel. She reached into the car, pulled two duffle bags from the back seat, and set them on the ground. Then she dived into the back seat and returned with a small, brown, beat-up briefcase.

"Let me helps you with them bags," Ms. Francis offered, grabbing both duffle bags from the ground and slinging them over one shoulder. "Come on now. I gots to get supper on the stove." She waddled her way down the gravel path and onto the first step of the porch. Janie followed, but something in her peripheral vision caught her attention. She saw movement pass through the cracks of the privacy fence. Someone or something was back there. It stopped her for a moment in her tracks.

"Come on, youngin'," Ms. Francis, already standing at the top of the wooden steps leading to the porch, snapped Janie's attention back. Janie crunched her way through the gravel to catch up to her.

"Hi, missy," echoed a high-pitched voice from a rocking chair by the front window as Janie entered the porch. There sat a petite elderly woman with hair as silver as chrome, her skin as pale as a powder puff as she held one of the calico cats in her lap. She looked like an old black-and-white photo cut out and repasted onto a color picture. *I did not see her when I pulled in the driveway.*

"Well, hello," Janie responded. "I'm sorry. I didn't see you sitting there."

"No one ever does," the old woman whispered. "My name is Ada."

"Hi, Ada." Janie smiled then looked at Ms. Francis, who looked annoyed that Ada was taking up her time.

"This here is my new helper, Ms. Ada. Her name is Ms. Janie," Ms. Francis explained in a loud tone as if Ada was hard of hearing. Ms. Francis threw her head toward the front door, motioning for Janie to follow. She opened the screen door and whispered back at Janie, "Crazy as a loon, that one."

"Nice to meet you, Ada." Janie gave a quick wave and followed Ms. Francis into the dim house.

Chapter 3

It was much cooler inside the old house. The smell of mothballs rolled around the room. The foyer stretched as big as a room itself with a staircase hugging the right wall and disappearing into the upper floors of the house. Only thing in the room besides the stairs was a brown cabinet from which an old rusty padlock dangled.

"Go on up, youngin'. You takes the room at the top of the stairs, to the left. It's got a screened-in porch that overlooks the tracks. You can smoke and not disturb the others. Can't be having my guests disturbed by no newcomers." Ms. Francis handed the two duffle bags over to Janie. "I's be in the kitchen gettin' supper started. When you gets settled in, ya come on down and help. Round that corner to the back of the house is where the kitchen is." She pointed, showing Janie which direction.

"Ok. Thank you," Janie said as she nodded. Besides, she was not in a hurry to face her sister or the only man she'd ever loved. She had given them time to raise their kids. Hell, the youngest, Shelly, should be off to college by now. And the last she had heard, thanks to running into Cheryl Mickelson in Atlanta last summer, Nathan had married and was trying to have his first child. *Cheryl always got Brea and me confused, and that day was not any different.*

Janie lugged her duffle bags and suitcase up the staircase. To the left, as Ms. Francis had instructed. Dropping the duffle bags to the hardwood floor, she opened the solid wooden door. The room was just as untouched as the rest of the house. Beautiful clusters of magenta verbena flowers spotted the wallpaper that wrapped around the room. The mothball aroma faded as Janie stepped through the doorway. The fragrant scent of clean sheets and lavender, complementing the flowered wallpaper, danced its way to her nose. It was funny how, since the accident, she noticed her senses were so much stronger than they ever had been. Smells were stronger, the sun was brighter, and the sounds of music were so much richer. She walked to the French doors leading out to the balcony that Ms. Francis referred to as a porch. It was facing the tracks, just as she had said. Janie could even see her car parked in the driveway below. She pulled her pack of cigarettes and her lighter from her front pocket. Taking a big draw as she lit one, she noticed an ashtray on a small table beside a chair. Janie smiled, thinking it was almost as if the room had already been set up for her stay.

Flower boxes filled with shades of blue and purple bellflowers sat around the railings of the porch. The house — obviously built in the early nineteen hundreds. Old southern-Florida homes were known for having porches to keep cool during the summer months. A rich sound of strumming floated through the slightly opened door and onto the porch and caught her attention. Putting out the cigarette in the ashtray, she followed the music through the doors and into the hallway. It lead her to a room, its door propped open with an old red brick.

"You play beautifully," Janie said, peeking her head into the doorway. On a wooden stool, there sat a man strumming an acoustic guitar. He looked a bit rough around the edges, but the music bellowing from the guitar cradled in his lap was as soft and soothing as a blanket in the cold. Tattoos ran the sleeve of his arm and were cut short at the top of his shoulders where his black t-shirt began.

He nodded and continued to strum. "If you are smoking in that room, Ms. Francis is gonna have your 'hind." He smiled through his facial hair.

"Oh... I was on the porch. I must have left the French doors open and the smoke... My apologies." Janie stepped farther into the room.

"Not a big deal to me. I love the smell of tobacco burning. I used to smoke. Quit a few years back. Brings back the memory of good times for me." He continued to strum and to finger the neck of the guitar.

"How long have you played?" she asked.

He stopped strumming and smiled again through the facial hair. "About thirty years. I think I got my first guitar just after I graduated from high school. I played a lot back then... But then I had to grow up for a while." A slight chuckle through the facial hair. "You know — get a job and make money to survive on my own. Then I would only play here and there. I lost my job at the factory and started playing again to get money. First on the streets, then I started getting a gig here and there. Been playing since."

"Wow! Hi, I'm Janie." She approached him with her hand out.

"Thomas." He shook her hand. "Are you the newcomer everyone has been talking about?"

"No, I don't think so. I just arrived no more than thirty minutes ago. I am originally from here. This town. I have a sister here... I just needed a room for a few days, a week max." Janie was silent for a moment. "My sister doesn't know I'm here yet." She looked down at the hardwood floors, ashamed. "It's been thirty years since I have been home."

"Where is you, youngin'? I needs ya!" traveled up the staircase and down the hall to Thomas' room where Janie stood.

"I'll be right down, Ms. Francis!" Janie yelled over her shoulder and turned back to Thomas. "Nice to meet you, Thomas."

"Nice to meet you, too, Janie." He resumed strumming his guitar. Janie listened as she backed her way out of the room.

"Woo woo, chicky." Large hands touched Janie's back, and she turned to see a tall, old, bald man standing in the hall. Thin as a rail, he was. He wore a white button-up shirt and trousers cinched with a shiny black belt. "Chicky, you best not keep Ms. Francis waiting. She doesn't like it when the newcomers keep her waiting." Straight-faced, he nodded.

"Yes, you are right," Janie answered, continued to the staircase, and began to descend. "I am Janie, by the way," she added, looking up at this tall old man now leaning over the railing, watching her.

"I know who you are, dear." With a nod and lips pursed, he smirked.

Chapter 4

Janie followed the smell of fried food and baked cornbread through the downstairs to find her way to the kitchen. Ms. Francis was right about a big house full of guests. As she walked into the old kitchen — oh, the amount of food, simmering and bubbling in pots. Janie stood, convinced; she was going to be running into many more guests.

Ms. Francis' back faced the entrance to the doorway where Janie paused. "Come on in, youngin'. Need to gets that cornbread crumbled up for the stuffing. Celery needs a cuttin', too." She turned the fried chicken in the cast-iron frying pan. Thin slices of eggplant and green tomatoes sat patiently on the counter, waiting to be battered and fried. Collard greens took a back burner next to the black-eyed peas. Both steamed out a succulent smell of fresh hickory-smoked bacon and ham hocks. One thing Janie had missed most about her small-town upbringing was the Southern soul food. During the years she had been gone, not once did she run across any food that compared. "Go ahead, child. Gots to get that cornbread stuffing in the oven before I gets started on the eggplant and tomatoes. Don't want them gettin' soggy before we eat."

Cornbread, baked fresh in cast-iron frying pans, lined the counter. A large stainless-steel bowl sat waiting.

"I'm not sure where to start." Janie approached the counter where the cornbread waited.

"Chop up the celery and onion. Gets that cornbread outta the pans; crumble it all up in the bowl. Mix 'em all up together — celery, onions, and cornbread. That little bowl has some fresh herbs and spices in it, mostly sage. Dump that in there, too." Ms. Francis waved her frying fork in the air as the spits and spatters of oil called for her attention. "Then gets that melted butter over there and drizzle it all over the cornbread mix. Can't never have too much butter in cornbread dressing." She pointed the fork and returned to frying.

"I got it." Janie began to chop the vegetables. Moments of steady work passed for her and Ms. Francis.

"Well hey, baby," Janie heard as she began to drizzle the butter onto some cornbread. She turned to see a small girl with cornrows and beads that matched the white dress with tiny red roses she wore. She never heard the little girl enter, but she now stood next to Ms. Francis, just staring up at the oil as it snapped in the pan. "I bets you's hungry." The little girl smiled and nodded in response, not saying a word. Ms. Francis looked over her shoulder at Janie and said, "This here's my grandbaby, little Annie. Her momma lives up the road. My daughter. This little one always knows when I gots food a cookin' in my kitchen." She hooked the last piece of fried chicken from the pan and stacked it onto the top of the pile she had already cooked. She wiped her hands on her apron before grabbing a large baking dish and handing it to Janie. "Dump that bowl in here, and let's gets that stuffing a bakin'."

"Hi, I'm Jamie. Nice to meet you, Annie," Janie said as she dumped the cornbread stuffing into the baking dish. The little girl tucked her head behind her grandma with only one eye peeking from around the apron as her grandma dipped the green tomatoes into the egg and then the flour. Janie smiled at the little girl as she walked the baking dish full of cornbread stuffing over to the preheated oven.

"I don't talk much to my daughter," Ms. Francis whispered to

Janie. "She's been hitting the bottle and don't want nothing to do with nobody." Then her voice gets a little louder. "But my sweet little Annie still comes to see me." She smiled and patted the top of the little girl's head.

Janie's face flatlined again as a memory of her days of drinking surfaced.

Janie's swollen, sticky eyes slowly opened as the whiskey bottle slid from her hand and hit the floor. Sporadic events of the night before flashed before her. Thank God she'd made it home alone this time. No annoying man to rid herself of this morning. Her studio apartment was not big enough for her, much less any company. A cockroach crawled from under the couch where she lay. The smell of Lug's Tavern had followed her home and lingered throughout the room. The taste of stale whiskey still saturated her mouth. The blur of her life dangled in her memory. It was time to have another drink.

"The cornbread stuffing. Check that cornbread stuffing!" Ms. Francis yelled over her shoulder as she added the eggplant to the hot oil. Janie made her way to the oven. Sure enough, the cornbread stuffing had turned gold-brown as hints of yellow peeked through.

"I think it is done, Ms. Francis," Janie said, grabbing two potholders and retrieving the baking pan. Ms. Francis and little Annie moved to the side of the stove so Janie could grab it from the oven. Dinner was almost ready; only the last three pieces of eggplant remained in the oil.

# # #

Janie stood staring at the long wooden table where Ms. Francis had asked her to place the plates on a thick, sturdy table that looked as old as the house. Well maintained and smelling of lemon-oil polish, there were wooden chairs that matched. Ten chairs waited patiently for the bodies to fill them. Could there possibly be ten guests staying here? She stared again at the china plates she held in her hand. There were ten. She began to place a plate in front of each seat and noticed a young lady, much younger than she was, standing in the doorway of the dining room. Dark eyes tried to see their way through the long black hair that fell in front of them. She did not say anything. Just watched as Janie set the table.

"Well, hello." Janie continued to set the table.

"That one never says a word," Ms. Francis interrupted, her hands balancing one platter of chicken and another filled with eggplant and tomatoes. "Been trying to get her to talk since she gots here. That's Nelly." She placed the platter of chicken onto the table as little Annie followed. "Stays up in her room mosts the time." Ms. Francis walked out of the room, babbling, to retrieve more food. As little Annie stayed, smiling at the platter of fried chicken, "Only comes down when she smells food a cookin'," came as a yell from the kitchen.

"Come on in. Food's ready. Go ahead — sit, Nelly," Janie said to the young woman and nodded toward the table as she placed the forks and knives next to the plates. As she set the silverware in front of the plate where little Annie stood, Janie softly said to her. "You are hungry, aren't ya?" Little Annie just grinned at Janie and shook her head. Janie could see little Annie wasn't so shy with her now, but this young lady looked like a challenge.

"I gots to warn you about Marva. Now, that one is as mean as a cottonmouth," Ms. Francis added as she entered the room.

"I am not." Marva stood in the doorway with hands on her hips and reading glasses hanging at the tip of her nose. A tall, thin woman with short, curly, salt-and-pepper hair. "I just don't take kindly to people. Especially people that invade my space." It appeared to be a warning as Marva stared at Janie.

"Understood." Janie nodded. Marva had definitely taken top of the totem pole now as being the challenger. Janie wondered what had she had gotten herself into.

Ms. Francis leaned down to little Annie. "Run on up and tell Thomas and Mr. Norman we's ready to have some supper." Then she added, "Hurry up now, ya here? Don't be lollygagging, little one."

Everyone began to sit, and Janie stood back, waiting to see

where her seat might be. The last thing she wanted was to sit in someone's spot or space, as Marva had put it. Little Annie returned. Thomas helped escort a smiling, disabled-looking teenage boy towards the table. The tall man from the hall, Mr. Norman, followed moments later.

"Hey there, little Tommy," Ms. Francis said to the disabled teen. "How's you feelin' today? Better, I hopes."

The teen just grinned at Ms. Francis as Thomas wiped the drool from the corners of Tommy's mouth.

After everyone had seated himself or herself, Janie noticed three chairs had remained empty. Therefore, she waited.

"Ada!" Ms. Francis yelled from the head of the table. "Crazy broad's probably took off again." She began serving up food to little Annie.

"Should I go check on her?" Janie offered to Ms. Francis.

"Naw, she be in," Ms. Francis mumbled as she cut up little Annie's fried green tomato. "That one's always wanting to be noticed. Wants us to make a fuss about her all the time." Ms. Francis added in a whisper, "You know, likes to make an entrance."

Janie still stood, not wanting to sit until all the chairs were filled.

"I'm here... I'm coming," Ada finally answered, moving sluggishly toward the table. She was an old woman and was obviously not as energetic as the rest of them were. Janie pulled out a chair for her. "Thank you, child," she said to Janie then whispered to Ms. Francis, "I like this one."

"Go on and sit now." Ms. Francis nodded to one of two seats left.

Janie sat and glanced at the empty seat next to her. "Are we expecting someone else?"

The table of guests became motionless, and silence spoke for a moment.

"That is for the newcomer. No telling when they gonna arrive," Ms. Francis finally answered then bowed her head. "Blessed we are for the food we are about to receive. In Jesus' name I pray. Amen." She began to gnaw on her chicken leg. The rest of the table joined her, and Janie began to serve herself, too.

Chapter 5

"Supper was fabulous," Janie mentioned as she assisted Thomas and Tommy up the staircase. "It's been years since I had a meal like that. I'm assuming Tommy's your boy?" Tommy just marveled at Janie. She smiled back at him.

"He is. I wasn't such a great dad in his early years. Trying to make up for it now." Janie listened as they reached the top of the staircase. "Back when I was gigging a lot, I met his momma. Oh, we had some good times, drank a lot back then. You name it, I did it. Pills, meth, heroine. Coke was my favorite, and his momma was right there with me. I was still able to have pride in my music."

Thomas guided Tommy into the room, pulled the door closed, and remained in the hall with Janie. "Well, probably why Tommy is the way he is. Both parents riddled with toxins," he calmly said through his facial hair. "Now after he was born, his momma cleaned up. Not me. I kept gigging and drinking and whatever else I could get my hands on." Thomas slid his hands into his pockets. "I'm clean now, and I want to make things right between me and my boy. Show some pride in him. Hell, he probably has no clue, either. It's not about him; it's about doin' what's right, ya know?"

Janie stood for a moment, not saying a word but remembering her reason for coming back home. *To make things right.* "I completely understand," she finally answered. "I suppose that is my mission, too, Thomas." Janie smiled. "Thank you for reminding me. You have a good night."

Janie headed to her room. The door was now closed and her bags no longer sat in the doorway. She opened the door to find her room still immaculate. She headed to the dresser and opened it, finding her clothes neatly put away. She opened the closet, and the duffle bags hung there neatly on hooks inside. Her small brown briefcase sat on the floor of the closet.

"I don't know how she does it," Janie mumbled, assuming Ms. Francis had somehow put all of her belongings away. She made her way to the French doors and opened them. The smell of fresh, Florida, summer air. There is no smell quite like it. An earthy dampness drifted above the lavender scent. After closing the doors behind her, Janie lit up a cigarette and noticed the ashtray had been dumped as well. A small chuckle rumbled in her throat as she took another drag. A firefly snapped in the midst of the darkness. Janie's thoughts of her childhood took over.

"Get it, Brea! Get it before it gets away!" Janie ran toward the lightning bugs, holding a mason jar in one hand and the lid in the other. "I got it!" Janie slapped the lid onto the jar. The two girls stood staring at the bug as it blinked its light, signaling its distress. It seemed as though the

other lightning bugs had disappeared in the darkness.

"Poor thing. We should let it go, Janie. He looks sad," Brea whispered, mesmerized by the captive bug.

"No, I want to keep it as a pet." Janie sealed the jar.

"He won't be able to breathe," Brea gasped, still staring at the jar. "He might miss his family..."

"I'll make things right first thing in the morning," Janie convinced herself after reviewing Thomas' conversation and the memory of the firefly. Her heart warmed at the thought of what that man was sacrificing for his boy. It had to be hard taking care of a disabled teen. The transitions Tommy must be going through, and still Thomas was determined to make things right. It was inspiring and encouraging.

Janie tapped out the cherry of her cigarette and stared at the evening stars. The crickets chirped as the moon brightened, as if the sound was pushing the movements of the clouds. Maybe this place, her hometown, was not so bad after all.

# # #

The train horn sounded, jump-starting Janie's heart as she sat up in the old four-post bed. The rumbling of the house as the train passed had woken Janie. It sounded as if the house was about to crumble on top of her. The walls of the old house moaned from the quaking of the earth. Although the night weather was calm, the wind from the train's passing rustled the leaves into a spout that danced across the yard.

Janie lay back down, listening to the echo of the train's voice screaming its arrival into her small town and whispering its way out. Just as she had begun on her own journey to return to this town — and hopefully to leave just as peacefully as that train. Things seemed to be calming her, helping her, and in a strange way to make it less scary.

The house was now calm and quiet. Janie lay silently, listening to the sound of nothingness, when she heard the sound of the downstairs door slamming. Footsteps thumped their way on the hardwood floors as if they were traveling up the staircase. The thumping stopped outside her door.

Janie sat up to see a shadow of feet streaking from the hall to stop under the door to her room. A moment passed, and they moved on. Janie wondered who it could have been. Everyone had returned to his or her own room as the night had begun to become apparent.

Sounds of silence covered the old house once again.

Chapter 6

Janie's eyes fluttered a moment as she slowly awakened from a deep sleep. She had slept pretty well, waking only once when the train had passed by at three a.m. She remembered the rumble of the house had startled her. Not to mention the train's loud horn blowing. Her momma had always said the horn was a warning the train was a coming. She sure wished she had gotten to see her momma and her daddy before they had passed. Brea had helped take care of them the last days of their lives.

As Janie sat up in bed, she noticed a hot cup of coffee and a biscuit with fresh butter waiting on a tray on her bedside table.

Again, she babbled to herself, "I don't know how she does it."

Janie smiled. It was nice having someone fuss over her like that. Maybe she should have gotten up a little earlier to help Ms. Francis — you know, to earn her keep.

As for Brea, she was always so nurturing. That was probably why Dillon had chosen her to be his wife. Taking care of everyone else and never expecting anything else in return. Like she enjoyed being "the good sister."

Animosity was Janie's biggest issue with her sister. Janie always felt like Brea did the whole "good sister" thing to show everyone that Janie was being selfish. She had to admit, at times she did want things her way. In addition, she fought to have it that way.

But maybe she had gotten it all wrong; maybe Brea just felt the need to care for people. A lot like Thomas' need to care for Tommy. Make things right. Like Ms. Francis, too.

Janie sipped the steamy coffee. *De-lish*. She set it back on the tray and stretched her arms. She sure felt good this morning, much better than the nights she had slept in her car outside of the Hardees she worked at. She had to give herself credit. It had been a real sacrifice to get back on her feet. After a month of working overtime, she had been able to get that studio apartment.

Janie made her way to the bathroom and stood at the sink,

staring into the mirror. She was ready to confront her sister and make things right. She even noticed the thought of it was not causing the hot flash to surface, unlike most days. *I can do this,* she thought.

Janie turned on the faucet, splashed her face with some water, and stared into the mirror. *I wonder if we still look alike.* She glanced at the counter and noticed her toiletries bag waiting patiently. As she pulled her toothbrush from the bag and brushed her teeth, Janie had to snicker again about Ms. Francis' efficiency.

After washing up and getting dressed, she decided to go out onto the porch to have a smoke and finish her coffee and biscuit. She opened the French doors, and the heat of the morning sun blasted her. The lavender scent lingered through the moistness in the air. Birds chirped out a morning tune. Janie stepped out, closed the doors behind her, and jiggled a smoke from her pack. She lit it and looked down at the train tracks below to see a squirrel scampering across them. *Survival.*

# # #

Janie made her way down the stairs and out the front door. As expected, Ada sat in the old rocker by the window with the same calico cat resting in her lap.

"Hi, Ada," Janie said just to let her know she noticed her. She continued down the steps, but half way to her car she heard Ms. Francis yell.

"Where you off to, girl? You can't leave yet. You gots chores to do." Janie looked up, noticing Ms. Francis' head poking out through one of the open upstairs windows. "Gots things here to take care of first before you go runnin' off."

"I'll be right up," Janie hollered back, opened the passenger car door, and threw her small briefcase onto the back seat.

As she returned to the house and began to jog up the stairs, Janie paused a moment, half way to the top, and looked back. Nelly stood below in the doorway of the foyer and sitting room, as Ms. Francis had called it. "Hi, Nelly," Janie called.

"My room," Nelly mumbled to Janie through her black hair. Janie was making headway with that one. Oh, how Ms. Francis would be proud she had gotten Nelly to speak! Janie smiled then continued her jog to the top of the stairs.

She entered Nelly's room to see Ms. Francis removing the bed's sheets while a pile of fresh sheets sat patiently folded on the nightstand.

"You's different from the rest of the guests, Janie." Ms. Francis rolled up the dirty sheet and threw it toward the doorway. "You's not staying here long. So you gots to earn your way."

"I understand." Janie grabbed the clean, fitted sheet from the table and began to spread it across the bed.

"You's more solid, if you gets what I'm sayin'." Ms. Francis added, "You still gots determination, life in ya that they don't gots no more." Ms. Francis tucked the fitted sheet under a corner of the bed then pointed to the top sheet. "They is all workin' on making things right in their own ways. And you... You still gots to make things right, too."

Oh, how Janie knew what she was talking about. It was her whole reason for coming back home. She grabbed for the sheet, but something slid and hit the hardwood floor. It must have come from the end table. A razor blade. Janie picked it up and stared at the blade in her hand.

"That girl's always a cutting on herself. Just put it back in the drawer." Ms. Francis seemed unconcerned.

A moment flashed. After she had gotten raped one night outside of Clancy's Bar, Janie herself had attempted to slice her own wrists. But the longing for revenge, the wrath she had felt for even entertaining the thought of killing herself, and the thought of the rapist getting the best of her had stopped her.

"She never goes through with it, just cuts herself enough to make a mess of my sheets," Ms. Francis continued. "You knows she can't even tell me why she does it, either."

"She spoke to me," Janie admitted. "On my way up."

Ms. Francis smiled. "She's a talkin'?" The smile grew. "You

knows what that means, don't ya? She's a makin' headway." Ms. Francis continued to make the bed, filling the pillowcases with pillows.

Moments passed as silence stood between them. "I is always a believer that no guest be stayin' for long before another one fills the spot." Ms. Francis began wiping the wooden furniture with lemon oil on a cotton rag. "Child, goes and gets that bathroom straightened up. Besides, where's you headin' off to today?"

"I grew up here. Left about thirty years ago. I'm going to see my sister. Things sure haven't changed, with the exception of the Cramers' old hotel — it's gone. And Old Man Dandy doesn't even own the gas station anymore," Janie said through the wall of the bathroom. "I never thought that was even a possibility."

"Nope. Son owns the place now. Mr. Dandy lost one of his grandbabies in some kind of gas fire; he went crazy. Poor baby was burned so bad they could not even have a viewing. He never gots that closure, ya see. So tell me, child, how's you find out about my place here?" Ms. Francis asked.

"Andy at the gas station. Mr. Dandy's grandson." Janie poked her head from the bathroom doorway. "He never mentioned why his grandpa didn't have the place anymore." She returned to cleaning.

"I sees... He's a good kid, that Andy. He, too, never gots that closure."

"He seemed fine to me," Janie said from the bathroom.

"I suppose he would to you, child," Ms. Francis mumbled.

"Now, that Andy," Ms. Francis answered, grinning, "comes by to sees me sometimes. Always brings his own pop, too." Ms. Francis chuckled then wiped down the windowsill. She paused and looked out the window. "Everybody gots things they need to take care of. Maybe that is why you's here. You gots to make things right," Ms. Francis said to the window for a moment before turning to face the room. "All we gots left is Mr. Norman's room, and you can go sees that sister of yours, but I's gonna need you back here before supper, ya hear?"

"Of course." Janie returned from the bathroom and scooped up the dirty sheets from the floor.

Chapter 7

Survival. Janie thought back to why she had done many of the things she was not proud of. If she had chosen to slice her own wrists, in a strange way it would have been an easy way out. Instead she chose to relive the terror of rape. She chose to face it and learn from it. In her own weird way, it made her see that no one could ever get the best of her.

It probably held true, in addition, for why she had left this town so many years ago. Maybe it was not the town after all — maybe she had taken the easy way out. She was a survivor; living on the streets had taught her that. She could have faced these people and learned from them just as she had done with the rapist. It would have been cake to survive any slander this town could have possibly fed her. However, in her own way, she gave Brea the life she had always wanted. Husband, family, and kids. Although it was her biggest regret, the dirty deed, the whole reason she had hauled ass, was not even close to being as bad as the many things she had done after leaving. She knew the truth and the consequence. Nothing else mattered.

Always so worried about being the black sheep, disappointing her parents, and making Brea out to be so perfect, Janie was far from perfect and so was this town's idea of what was perfect. Nothing is perfect; that she *did* know. That was why she had left, the fear of disappointing everyone she'd ever loved and of revealing the truth about this town's idea. Maybe she did what she did to keep what little bit of Dillon she had gotten for herself — his desire to see the world. As for Brea, she always did the right thing, almost as if it just came natural to her. Janie honestly always despised that fact. It angered her at times how life seemed so effortless to Brea.

As she coasted her car down River Street, noticing all of the prestigious homes that lined the waterway, envy struck her again. This time, today, there was also a sense of pride she could not explain. She felt envy coming from the people jailed by what society thought was right — or normal. She was able to see the world. She was not confined to small-town gossip and caged ambitions. She struggled, sure, but she also saw now how stagnant her town was, how it had not changed in thirty years. She'd had to leave back then because she was inevitably changing. She'd needed to grow, to expand. It was in her veins, the need to see the world. For some odd reason, today was the first time she ever saw exactly why her life had happened the way it did. The idea of being stagnant was far worse than any hardship she had already gone through.

She arrived at Brea's and Dillon's home, its white picket fence and shrubs perfectly square to the green grass that blanketed the lawn. An autumn-colored stone-pavered sidewalk lead to the stoop that blended into the doorway. A makeshift ramp stretched along half of the stoop out front. The home was beautiful and was everything a good sister like Brea deserved. *Am I ready for this?* Janie asked herself again as she pulled her car into the driveway paved to match the sidewalk.

She climbed from her car and hesitated in the driveway. Janie noticed the plywood ramp, obviously added recently. She approached the stoop; it too was decorated with autumn-colored bricks. She graciously stepped one step at a time. The welcome mat at the door finally greeted her. It was a sign to her that no matter what, she was going to make things right. The doorbell rang from her fingertips as if something or someone else had done it. Nevertheless, it was her own action.

Moments of nothingness passed. Then there she was, Brea, standing in the doorway, staring at Janie. To Janie, it was more like staring through her. Looking out past her.

"Hi..." Janie exhaled. No response from Brea, only a slight acknowledgement that Janie had arrived. Brea looked tired, not at all as Janie had expected. Saddened but not with a sadness she had caused. In that moment, Janie realized, maybe Brea needed her. Maybe not everything she knew of her sister was at all who she was. Maybe she'd had some kind of hardship. Brea was just like the prestigious homes caged by a lack of life. Beautiful but desolate. But Brea's cage was the one she had built herself.

"Can I come in?" Janie asked.

Brea solemnly walked away from the opened doorway. Janie entered to find the home seemed just as solemn. She noticed how she and her sister still looked very much alike. Even their hairstyles were similar. Only Brea's was salon-maintained and Janie's hair was in great need of an inch or two taken off. At fifty years old, they still had a youthfulness about their styles. Brea was always the more conservative dresser, with all the latest name brands. Still, there was something about her eyes; they looked less innocent than they once did. Brea was a grandma now, Janie could see by the baby toys placed in different areas of the room.

"I know you are probably wondering why I'm here," Janie began as Brea stood, facing away from Janie in front of the beautiful stone fireplace, staring at her family portrait as Janie approached her. "I just felt a need to come here and make things right between us again..." As Janie walked around to look her sister in the eyes, she noticed Brea had tears running down her cheek. "Oh Brea, I'm so sorry for what I did."

"I-don't-need-this!" Brea yelled, throwing her hands in the air before she ran out of the room. A moment later, the sound of a slamming door followed her. Silence struck, and the knot in Janie's throat grew. She had known Brea would not welcome her back with open arms. She'd prepared herself for what had just happened. But even so, she was a step closer. Brea could just as easily have slammed the door in her face, but she had not. She welcomed her into her home, although the doormat was the only one who had spoken. Brea's gestures had welcomed her, and that was good enough. She could have screamed for her to leave then. However, she had not. She had at least given her time to speak.

Janie looked at the pictures stretched across the fireplace mantel. The love of a family. Brea's and Dillon's wedding pictures. The births of their son and daughter. At the far end was an old picture of Janie and Brea in matching dresses, before Dillon had moved to town. Her sister still had hope in the two of them or the picture would not have been there. The picture was before all the animosity and jealousy, when they were sisters and took care of one another, Janie noticed.

"She won't speak to me, either." Dillon's voice startled her. "It has been at least a week since she even spoke my name. She just lays around. The doctor gave her some medicine to help her feel better, but if you ask me, it has made her worse. Not eaten a whole lot either. I'm worried about her, Janie." He began a smile from the doorway of the living room. "It's been years. How have you been?"

Janie for a moment stared at Dillon. He rolled across the floor in a wheelchair. "What happened? I mean... How?" She stared at the chair. "I'm sorry, I just wasn't expecting..."

"Midlife crisis," he chuckled. "That's what happened. I had some crazy notion I could be that youthful daredevil I used to be. As you see, it got the best of me," he said as he rolled up to the mantel where Janie stood and looked up at the wedding pictures. "Seems it got the best of your sister, too."

"I'm sorry. I didn't know..." Janie paused. "I shouldn't have come..." She began to back up.

"Don't be silly." He spun the wheelchair around. "Nothing is ever by accident. I know it seems like we are going through a rough time, but hey, can't always be perfect. Your sister needs you, and if my gut is right, you need her."

"I'm not sure why I'm here." Janie glanced around the room, not sure what she should do. "I just woke up one day and some force pushed me out the door and into my car. Repeatedly, I heard I needed to make things right with my sister. The strange thing is, the voice I heard was Brea's. I really didn't want to come." She stepped back toward the door. "I felt that I was supposed to. I also have a crucial need to tell you something important." Janie stood still and bowed her head. "I know I just up and left. I never explained why, and of all people, you deserve to hear it."

"I loved you, Janie." Dillon's expression changed. "But things have changed. Brea is my wife, I love her deeply, and we have kids.

And for God's sake, Janie, we have a grandchild now." It was apparent Janie had struck a nerve. "So now you want to make things right? Brea was right — she doesn't need this." He began to leave the room but stopped when Janie spoke.

"No, you don't understand. I'm not here to cause more pain. I'm here..." Janie surrendered. "I'm here to get my sister back."

Frustrated, Dillon rolled out of the room. "Good luck with that."

Chapter 8

They needed time. All they both needed was time — time to cool down. It was a shock to see her sister and Dillon after all of these years. Janie was ready, but maybe they were not. That was apparent. If Janie could show up at any point in their lives, it had to be now. Midlife crisis. Janie was certain things were not going so well for the two of them. After all of the animosity and jealousy she'd held for her sister, you would think a small amount of happiness would surface, but it had not. Sadness was what she had felt not only for her sister but also for Dillon. She would return tomorrow.

She would return every day until things were right between them.

Janie pulled into the gravel driveway of Ms. Francis' big old yellow house. She reached into the back seat of the car and grabbed for her battered briefcase. She sat it in her lap and opened it. She shuffled the papers she had in it around to find a prescription bottle. Her medication. The pills the doctor had prescribed for her when depression had hit her the hardest. It had been months since she had taken them. She kept the full bottle as a safety net. A *just in case*. Today was a day that borderlined between anxiousness and breaking down in tears. For a moment, she considered popping one of the capsules into her mouth. Only to take the edge off; her emotions were so shaky. So she did and then returned the bottle to her briefcase.

She stared ahead at the tall wooden fence. Something was damn sure behind it, and it was something the rest of the world need not see. Much the way she thought of her own life adventures. Why hadn't anyone spoken of the back yard? None of the guests mentioned it. Not even Ms. Francis. As a matter of fact, no one even spoke of leaving this place. She was the only one remotely considering staying only for a short time. *Odd*, Janie thought.

She climbed over the stick-shift and out of the car. She grabbed for her pack of cigarettes, tapped one out, and lit it. Oh, how her sister Brea hated the smell of smoke. She thought back...

"Why are we hiding under here?" a thirteen-year-old Brea asked Janie.

"I wanna grab one of Daddy's cigarettes. He is almost done smoking, so he'll leave his pack on that table and go back in the house. He always does after dinner," young Janie said, peeking through the wooden floorboards of the porch, watching her father exhale the smoke as if all his worry floated off with it.

"Why would you want one of Daddy's cigarettes? They smell something awful," Brea whispered back to her sister.

"I think they smell wonderful. They have to taste just as good, or *why would he smoke them every night after he eats?"*

"Momma says those things will kill ya." Brea warily peeked through the same hole. Janie was so much like her Daddy: adventurous and always looking for the greener grass. As for Brea, she was the spitting image of her mother: content and happy, admiring the bed she had made.

Janie stomped the cigarette out. Brea was always a voice of reason, even back then. Brea never wanted to do bad things. She just watched as Janie made all the mistakes. And Janie sure knew she had made her share of mistakes. She proceeded down the gravel path to the porch to find Ada still sitting where she had left her earlier. "Hi, Ada."

"Janie? I wasn't sure you were coming back so soon." Ada rocked in the chair. There was something different about Ada. Not so black and white today. Like she wore a hint of pink added to her lips, and her dress looked as if it wanted to fade to a purple-blue color. Janie stood trying to figure out quite why. Maybe her meds were starting to kick in. Maybe Ada was glowing because someone was actually beginning to notice her. Janie shook the thought away.

"Oh, it is looking like I'll be here for some time, Ada. Some things I need to take care of are just going to take me a little longer than I was expecting."

"They always do, my dear, they always do." Ada rocked in the chair as she glided her hand across the calico cat's back.

The other cats still lay lazily among the railings of the porch. Just to stir up some conversation, Janie asked, "How many cats do you think Ms. Francis has here?"

"Cats? Oh honey, those aren't Ms. Francis' cats, those are my babies." Ada answered as any old woman would. Strangest thing was, Janie knew Ada really believed they were her babies. Ms. Francis was right about Ada; she was on the crazy side. "This here is Jeffy. He is my youngest," Ada whispered. "Always needing all the attention..."

Janie questioned herself for a moment. Did she, too, always need all the attention? Was she the sister lashing out or acting out to be noticed? Could that have been another reason she'd left? To be noticed? Brea had always been in her shadow, not once wanting to be seen.

"You's back!" Ms. Francis' dark figure said through the screen door. "Good thing. I needs help in my kitchen. Little Annie come by and been a beggin' for some brownies. I gots that a goin', but now it's coming on to be suppertime and I ain't even close to gettin' it started."

"Sure thing. I'm here now. We will have supper ready in a jiffy." Janie smiled at Ada then glanced at Ms. Francis.

"Yummy! My babies love homemade brownies," Ada mumbled as she rocked.

# # #

The kitchen smelled of gooey chocolate-fudge brownies as they cooled on the counter. "We's gonna have breakfast for supper tonight." Ms. Francis knelt down and tapped little Annie on the nose. "Sounds yummy, don't it, little one?" Little Annie just smiled her precious smile. Ms. Francis hollered over her shoulder at Janie. "How's you at rolling out biscuits, child?"

"I suppose I can handle that," Janie replied and turned to the counter where the dough sat in a stainless-steel bowl. A rolling pin sat next to the biscuit cutter.

"I gots the dough over yonder, ready for rolling. Just sprinkle some flour on the counter and gets going on that. Don't forget to add some shortening to that pan. Can't have my biscuits all stuck down. There's a headache — tryin' to unstick a biscuit," Ms. Francis coached. "I's goin' to get started on the sausage gravy. Annie, gets Gram the milk from the fridge and grabs me the bacon, too. After that, I's gonna need the eggs, sweetie."

"Ms. Francis?" Janie asked. Curiosity had finally gotten the best of her. "What's in the back yard? I mean, you have quite a bit of property, but your back yard is like it is sealed off from the rest of the world." Janie chuckled, knowing damn well her imagination was not going to stop until she had an answer.

"That back yard is none of your concern, child." Ms. Francis stared wide-eyed back at Janie.

Janie swallowed hard. Had she overstepped her boundaries? She was only curious. What could possibly be the big deal? Why would someone like Ms. Francis be so protective of a back yard, anyway? "You stay away from that back yard—ya hear me, child?" Ms. Francis glared.

"No problem." Janie began rolling the dough out. The heat of her embarrassment began to rise. Why would she react like that? She'd meant no harm. Now her curiosity grew even stronger. "I just thought maybe there was a swimming pool back there or a garden. I didn't mean to sound as if I was prying," Janie confessed.

"Like I says, you stay away from that back yard." Ms. Francis nonchalantly continued to prepare the sausage gravy. "Ain't got no pool. Ain't got no garden. If you wantin' to knows what's back there so bad, take care of your business with your sister first. Then and only then, I's gonna let you back there," she babbled as she grabbed the bacon and milk from little Annie. "How did it go for you, today?" Ms. Francis smiled as if her frustration had gone as quickly as it had shown. She obviously was trying to change the subject.

Janie swallowed to wash away the knot that had lodged in her throat. And to move on from the subject. "She wouldn't speak to me, but I don't know. I feel like she still wants me there. She just isn't ready to face me yet."

"Probably havin' to deal with her own issues. Like I says, child, we all's got to make things right in our own time, in our own ways."

Ms. Francis poured in the milk and stirred the thickening gravy. Little Annie just watched as the scent of morning danced around the kitchen and the sweetness of brownies framed the evening.

Janie wanted badly to ask Ms. Francis about her daughter. She knew things must not have been so great between them. Little Annie always seemed to be around.

However, she was certainly not going to ask that question today, especially after Ms. Francis had gotten all bent out of shape about the back yard. Ms. Francis seemed to tell it like it was, but it was obvious she had secrets of her own.

Chapter 9

"Breakfast for dinner?" Marva snarled as she pulled the chair from the table and took a seat. "I have never..."

"Marva, you never gots nothing nice to say. Sit, woman, and eat. It's a gettin' cold." Ms. Francis shuffled along, carrying a basket of hot biscuits from the kitchen. "Go on, Janie, you sits, too." She nudged her head toward the two empty spots left at the table.

Thomas and Tommy sat directly across from her. Ada had already come in and was scooping scrambled eggs onto her plate. Nelly, too, sat next to little Annie and actually had one barrette pinning some of the hair from her eyes, but they were still unable to be seen.

Of course, Mr. Norman, as tall as he was for an old man, seemed to always grab the head of the table opposite from where Ms. Francis sat. Once again, the newcomer's place was set but no one occupied the space. Janie kind of wondered to herself if maybe it was set for Ms. Francis' daughter. Maybe Ms. Francis hoped her daughter would someday join them. Could be why it always had to be set. It did seem like little Annie was always around.

"We says blessings first." Ms. Francis waved her hand, stopping Ada from taking a mouthful of eggs. Ms. Francis sat and bowed her head. "Blessed we are for the food we are about to receive. Thank you, Lord, and may you have mercy on Marva; she means nothing by her meanness. In Jesus' name I pray. Amen."

"The brownies smell fabulous." Marva smirked at Ms. Francis as she waved a crunchy piece of bacon. Janie pondered a moment. She had never noticed that Marva had a beautiful smile. And she was right: the brownies did smell fabulous. Little Annie ate a bit of her biscuits and gravy while still patiently anticipating one of those brownies, Janie noticed.

Janie took bites of her food, and the flavors exploded in her mouth. She had not realized she was as hungry as she was.

For a moment, she felt as though she was spinning although the room sat still. All of the guests continued eating, not noticing. Could she be having some weird reaction to her meds? She sipped some water. The feeling seemed to be going away as fast as it had arrived, until the chatter at the table had changed to musical tones highlighted with ringing laughter. Something was happening to her. As she glanced around the table, everyone's face moved closer to her and then moved back again. Janie knew she had not moved. This time she picked up the orange juice. Maybe her blood sugar was low.

"You's pale as a ghost, child." Ms. Francis' distorted face appeared in front of Janie. "You all right, child?"

Darkness...

"We have her back. Keep moving."

The gurney pushed through the emergency-room doors. The babbling of frantic workers popped in the darkness.

"It's a code red..."

Janie could feel the pulling and pressure of her rib cage as she gasped for air. Pain... She could not feel her legs, and her body lay, moist in the saturated bed. She gasped for air.

Janie gasped for air again, sitting up this time. She was in her room with a wet rag on her forehead.

"You give me a scare, child. I knows Marva wasn't so keen on breakfast for dinner, but I's quite sure you were okay with the idea."

Ms. Francis stood by her bed, hands on hips. "You's feelin' better now?"

"I think so... What happened?" Janie scooted her bottom back to sit up a little better and to see if the room was still spinning.

"I thinks you passed out. I was a talkin' to ya one minute, and the next your eyes rolled back in your head. Mr. Norman and Thomas helped me get ya up the steps. Your color came back." Ms. Francis scanned Janie's face. "Ms. Marva use to be a nurse before she retired. She said you just passed out. She said probably all the worry over your sister. Then she told me it was 'cause you ain't supposed to be eatin' breakfast for supper. That when I knew you's be okay and it wasn't nothing serious." Ms.

Francis grabbed the washrag and took it to the bathroom to run water on it. She squeezed it out and returned. "Here, put it back on your head and try to rest some."

Janie sat a moment, trying to figure out why the memory of her accident had felt as though she was going through it again. Even the pelvic pain seemed so real. The smell of the hospital's disinfectant even seemed to linger in her nostrils. *Seemed so real...*

# # #

"I can't stop the bleeding... Hurry! We need to get her to the O.R. now!" a frantic voice yelled over the rumbling of the gurney. Janie gasped for air...

Janie woke at three a.m. with the rumbling of the train shaking the house right on schedule. She had been dreaming again about the aftermath of her accident. She was feeling much better now, although the slight shaking of the house had her wondering for a moment.

She got up and walked into the bathroom. Noticing her reflection in the mirror, she lifted her hair just a bit, tucking the ends under as if she wore a salon-styled bob. After seeing her sister again after so long, she realized even more so that she did look a lot like Brea.

Janie thought again about her safety-net meds. She remembered the doctor saying it would take a few doses to get everything balanced. She went out to her room and opened the closet where she had put the briefcase when she had arrived home. Yes, it was beginning to feel like a home. Before Ms. Francis had her rolling dough and began jumping down her throat about the damn back yard, anyway.

She opened the closet. All of her clothes were packed in her duffle bags and no longer hanging neatly in on the rod. Beside the duffle bags sat her old briefcase.

"Hmmm, that's strange." She had not packed the bags, but neither had she unpacked them. In addition, why would Ms. Francis pack them? She picked up the case and opened it to find the bottle of meds. Grabbing the bottle, she realized it sounded empty and gave it another shake. No rattle of pills. She opened the bottle to be sure. Empty.

There was no possible way. She had only taken one. The bottle had been full. Suddenly, she was startled by heavy footsteps in the hall. The same footsteps that always seemed to follow the train. Had she only stayed the one night? For some strange oddity, it was as if she was almost becoming quite content in this big yellow house. Like time had passed. A strange feeling of a paradox. Had she been here longer than she had thought? She felt fine tonight, but something — everything — was different. Even the pajamas she was wearing.

A sudden knock at the door frightened her. Putting the bottle back in the bag, she made her way to the door and slowly cracked it open enough to peek out to see who it was.

"You haven't come out in days. Are you going to be all right?" Ada stood in her nightgown that was blue as the sky and matched her eyes. Her skin was now a warm beige tone unlike her pale, nearly white complexion as on the day when Janie had arrived. Ada's lips, now pink as a melon in the summer, were different even than the hint of pink they had been earlier that day.

"What day is it?" Janie whispered.

"It's Monday. Early Monday morning."

"No, I'm positive it is Friday. I got here Wednesday, and today should be Friday. The sun should be rising in a couple of hours."

"No, dear, it is Monday." Ada looked down at her nightgown. "I know because this is my Monday gown." She curtsied for Janie.

Janie was not going to argue. Besides, Ada was a little on the senile side. "Ada, I'm fine. I was just needing to rest," she lied but for good reason. "Go get back to bed. I'll see you first thing in the morning." Janie slowly closed the door. "Good night."

What was happening to her? In addition, where had her medicine gone? She sure needed a cigarette.

She made her way out through the French doors and onto the porch. In the ashtray, cigarettes overflowed. Not one of the guests smoked. Only she smoked. Had she smoked all of those cigarettes and not realized it? She looked down at her car in the driveway, in the same place she had parked it — today, she reminded herself. Below, she heard a noise coming from the side of the house, the side where the gate for the fenced-in back yard stood. She watched in the darkness. A second later, a shadowy figure darted across the lawn and over the tracks. Something about the shadowy figure, the way it jogged off, seemed familiar.

The figure disappeared down the road that lead to the river. Janie rubbed her eyes. Was she seeing things? She exhaled, brought the cigarette to her lips, lit it, and took a drag. The cigarette did not taste the same. She put it out. Janie needed to rest, she thought, just as she had told Ada. *I'll see clearer in the morning.*

Chapter 10

The smell of fried fish lured Janie from her sleep. When she opened her eyes, she saw her clothes had been neatly put away. The ashtray had even been dumped. Nothing was the same as it had been last night. Following the mouth-watering aroma, Janie made her way down the stairs and entered the kitchen. Ms. Francis stood, frying fish in a cast-iron skillet.

"You need help?" Janie offered. If Ada was right, Ms. Francis had been having to prepare dinner without her.

"Oh hey, child... I was startin' to gets worried about you. You haven't touched breakfast or the lunch I brought ya. You gots to eat."

"Breakfast? Lunch?" Janie moved further into the kitchen.

"You slept right through the day. Ada was worried sick about ya, too. She says you told her you's be down today, this morning." Ms. Francis battered another piece of fish in the cornmeal-and-flour mix. She placed it in the snapping oil.

"Granny Fran, what's for supper?" little Annie asked as she entered the room. That was the first time Janie had heard the child speak, which jolted Janie for a moment.

"Catfish, grits, and fresh-snapped green beans, little one. Go wash up now, ya hear?" Ms. Francis told little Annie. After Annie had left the room, she said to Janie,

"That little one sure can eats; I just can't seem to fill her up. A glutton she is."

"I haven't been feeling so well... I guess." Janie rubbed her temples as she finally explained why she had not eaten. "Probably why I haven't been hungry. I usually have a hearty appetite."

She either was imagining all the weird things or dreaming them. Maybe the long road trip, which now seemed like a blur, just had her exhausted. She proceeded to finally tell Ms. Francis of the strange occurrences she had been experiencing. "Last night, I woke when the train went through. My clothes were packed in my bags, and then I went out to have a smoke on the porch — "

"Child, ain't no train going through; they stopped running them tracks ten years ago," Ms. Francis butted in.

Janie stood a moment, shocked. Had she been imagining the train going by every night? Maybe what she saw, the shadowy figure coming from the back yard, was her imagination, too? "Ms. Francis, I could have sworn I saw my sister here last night. Coming from the fence gate to the back yard. She ran across the tracks and down the road to River Street. It was dark, but I know I recognized her. At least I think I did..."

Ms. Francis just stopped everything she was doing, her back still facing Janie. It was the first time Ms. Francis had been silent for more than a minute. In a deeper voice, Ms. Francis said, "I told you, child, that back yard is no concerns to you." She swiftly turned to Janie. "Do ya hear me?"

"I do; I'm sorry. I haven't been myself. I haven't been myself in days. I just think that maybe my mind is playing tricks on me. Maybe I'm just... Never mind," Janie surrendered once again.

Ms. Francis handed Janie a pot of grits and in her normal voice said, "Gets these grits salted and buttered up. Put them in that bowl and get the table set." She sealed her lips, and the corners slowly turned to a grin or a smirk. "Go on, gets going now. We needs to get some food in ya. You's already skinny as a rail." She turned her back again to Janie. "Grab some of that cheddar cheese over yonder, too. Marva likes having cheese on her grits." Then she mumbled, "Woman ain't never satisfied with what she got."

Janie did what Ms. Francis asked. First, she buttered and salted the grits and scraped them into the pretty bowl with scalloped handles, its blue birds circling the steaming, buttered grits. *I think my mother had a bowl like this one*, Janie thought.

As she carried the plates to the dining room, other thoughts filled her attention. What was happening to her? She could not even trust her own mind anymore, whereas she had always depended on her inner thoughts with whatever life had thrown at her. Now she felt as though her inner thoughts were deceiving her. *The empty bottle of medicine*, she remembered. *Maybe they are giving me a different reaction this time.* Maybe it was she herself who had taken all of the pills.

"Well hello," said Mr. Norman, who was already seated at the empty table. Janie had not even noticed him when she walked in. "You haven't been around much."

"Oh hello, Mr. Norman. I have been here — just catching up on some greatly needed rest, I suppose," Janie answered the best she could.

"I envy you, you know." Mr. Norman sat back in his seat as Janie placed the china in front of him.

"Envy me? Why is that?"

"You can just up and go as you please. You are the age I was when

I found my lovely Ellen. Those were some of the best years of my life. You have your whole life in front of you, right now, and the wisdom to enjoy it. It's a very important time period."

"What do you mean? Your life isn't over. You could still get out and experience new things," Janie encouraged but realized she could have easily chosen to live a life like Brea and Dillon had lived.

"Oh honey, I'm too set in my ways now." Mr. Norman then whispered, "If you know what I mean..."

Strange. Janie just smiled at Mr. Norman. She continued to set the table, and he continued to talk about Ellen, how he would meet her again in the new world. Then Janie looked up to see Nelly standing in the dining-room doorway. Two barrettes today, Janie noticed. Nelly's eyes were a beautiful almond shape. It was apparent that Nelly had Oriental heritage. Almond eyes and thin lips.

"Come on in, Nelly. Supper is almost ready," Janie said and could almost see a slight smile come onto Nelly's face. She was becoming more social even if it was only a barrette at a time and a slight turn of her thin lips. *Two words and two barrettes,* Janie thought. *Progress.*

"That one never talks," Mr. Norman said. "I don't think she speaks English."

"That's not true. I have spoken with Nelly," Janie said to Mr. Norman then gave a wink back at

Nelly. A smile emerged from Nelly's thin lips.

"Where are you from, Mr. Norman?" Janie asked for no particular reason. Maybe it was just to have conversation other than hearing about how he envied her.

"Nebraska. Have you ever been to Nebraska?" he asked, not letting Janie answer the question. "Too cold for me there, now. My bones can't take it anymore. My children and their families are still there. Not me. My Ellen and I moved here to Florida just for that very reason."

After hearing about Ellen and how Mr. Norman would "meet her in the new world," Janie came to the conclusion that Ellen had passed on. Poor Mr. Norman was a widower, and now he was lost in a life of routine.

"I have to say Nebraska is one of the few places I have never been, Mr. Norman. And I have been all over. I might have to put that one on my bucket list," Janie chuckled, knowing damn well she had no desire to see Nebraska.

"Don't bother. I hated it there," he countered. "What are we having for dinner?"

"Fried catfish, grits, and fresh-snapped green beans." Ms. Francis came from the kitchen, balancing a platter of fried catfish and a platter of bright-green, buttered beans. "Oh, and hush puppies, too," Ms. Francis remembered. "Baby, run in the kitchen and grab the plate of hush puppies," she said to little Annie.

"Ada! Come on, woman!" Ms. Francis yelled as she placed the platters on the table. The dining room filled one by one with all of the guests. Once again, the tenth chair sat with no body to occupy it.

# # #

As the sun began to rise, Janie stood on the porch, sipping a cup of steamy coffee Ms. Francis must have just made. Janie had found it waiting on her bedside table when she woke. It amazed her how that woman was so on the ball and able to get the tray in Janie's room without waking her. She'd slept well last night and even though Ms. Francis was certain the train stopped running the tracks ten years ago, Janie was sure she'd felt its rumbling again. She decided she was just going to let it be. Surely an explanation would surface.

Janie noticed a faint knock at her door. She set the coffee cup next to the ashtray on the small table on the porch and entered through the French doors. The tapping started again just as she began to open the door. There, standing with an odd look on her face, was Marva.

"I want to give you this." With a very stern face, Marva grabbed Janie's hand and dumped from her own cupped hand what appeared to be a gold chain. "I always wanted a sister so we could wear matching chains..."

Janie opened her hand to see two chains with dangling little rose charms that were identical.

"Wow, Marva! How thoughtful of you," Janie said, admiring the delicate designs.

"I was an only child," Marva added. "Probably why I'm not much on sharing things." Still straight-faced, Marva continued, "Give one to your sister and maybe she will come around." A small turn of the corner of Marva's mouth showed Janie that Marva did actually have a sensitive side.

"I will give it to her today, after I help Ms. Francis out this morning. Thank you." Janie added, "You are up early. I thought I was the only one up."

"I haven't slept well in days." Marva turned away then

mumbled, "Just make sure your sister gets the necklace."

Janie whispered, "I sure will," as she stood in the doorway of her room. After Marva walked away, Janie put one of the beautiful necklaces around her neck. She turned and strolled into the bathroom, glancing at the mirror and placing her hand on the necklace as she twirled the rose charm in her fingertips. She thought back to the moment she'd decided she was leaving town.

"What are you doing?" Brea asked as she entered the bedroom they shared. They were twenty years old and still living at home. That was the thing to do — stay home until you found a husband or had a prosperous career. "Why are you

packing clothes? Are you going somewhere?" Brea stared over Janie's shoulder, watching as Janie appeared frazzled and frustrated.

"I can't take this life of being stagnant, Brea. I will never be a career woman, and you know it. I have no desire to get married. Mom and Dad are never going to let me out of here without some kind of financial security." Janie continued to pack.

"What about Dillon?" Brea asked. Janie stopped in her tracks and exhaled.

"He doesn't know I'm going." Janie turned to face her sister. "I broke it off with him last night. He told me I needed to figure it out." She threw her arms in the air. "I told him I wanted to see the world, travel, and experience *life. I don't want to be held down. Besides, no one will even notice I'm gone."* Janie turned back and continued to pack.

"I will," Brea softly muttered.

Janie quickly turned to another knock, this one more aggressive and energetic than Marva's, at her bedroom door. She exited the bathroom and answered the knock by opening the door.

"You's up, child?" Ms. Francis stood, bright-eyed, ready to take on duties. "I's hoping you'd be ready to help me get Ada's room together this morning."

"Oh sure... I was up early this morning just for that reason. I was hoping to go to my sister's again by this afternoon," Janie said as she nodded.

"You is a dear, child. Meet me in Ada's room in about ten minutes. I's goin' to go gets the clean sheets. She done had all them damn cats in her room again." Ms. Francis turned to leave. "Going to needs to get all that cat hair swept up off that floor, too. Crazy woman."

Moments later, Janie swigged down her coffee, quickly made her own bed, and headed out to help Ms. Francis. As she moved down the hall, she noticed Ada's door was open and Ms. Francis was already at work. The amount of color that painted the room was more than your average. Purple, red, hot-pink, and fluorescent-green boas hung from every corner of the room. It was almost as if Ada hoped being surrounded by so much color was going to make her less black and white. Although over the course of the week, it seemed she actually was filling in with color. "Oh my goddess!" Janie was mesmerized.

"That woman's done pushed me to my limit. I told her to keep them damn cats out of my house." Ms. Francis swept cat hair cross the floor.

"She's such a sweet woman. Don't be so hard on her," Janie snickered.

"She ain't so sweet, child. That woman just wanting to rally me up. Always trying to get my blood boiling." Ms. Francis swiftly scooped up the tumbleweed of hair.

"Why all the boas?" Janie's curiosity surfaced in the conversation.

"Well, Ms. Ada, back in her day, was always looking for men's attention. All men's attention, if you gets what I'm saying. She entertained them, if you gets my drift."

"What? Ada? I can't believe she..." Janie stood, dismayed.

"She was..." Ms. Francis' white eyes met with Janie's. "She was good at it, from what she told me. Sad thing is, all she ever was a wanting was a man to love her and give her a child. She ain't gots no family. All she gots is them damn cats."

"Still, you shouldn't be so hard on her." Janie quickly dunked into a memory of her own. A memory of her days of being promiscuous.

"Hey there, handsome." Janie exhaled the smoke slow and easy. "Whiskey, please," she yelled to the bartender and turned to face the man seated at the bar. She wanted him; as to why, probably part loneliness, but tonight she decided it was more about the challenge. In addition, to see how much money she could persuade out of him. Even if it was only footing the bill for the drinks and possibly breakfast if she decided to take him to her apartment.

"I got that," the man insisted to the bartender as he poured her a shot.

"Thanks." Janie smiled as she lifted the shot glass to her mouth.

She hesitated, the shot right at her lips, still staring deeply at the man as he turned his stool toward her. Janie licked her lips and slid the shot glass across her bottom lip, just splashing hints of whiskey to flavor them.

"Child. Help me with that corner." Ms. Francis flapped the fitted sheet across the bed and began tucking in the corners.

"Where is Ada originally from?" Janie's curiosity about Ada seemed apparent.

"Louisiana. Baton Rouge, if I'm remembering right," Ms. Francis replied.

"I lived in Baton Rouge for a time." Janie remembered well.

"She ain't always been there. She actually lived up the road for a time. She'd get all dressed up in her fancy attire and sit out on the porch waiting on the trains to pass back when they was still running them tracks. Almost as if she was waiting on a specific man to show up, but all she gots was cats. Now she done brought them to my house. Every morning I wake up, there's another stray on my porch." Ms. Francis threw a cotton rag at Janie and nodded to the lemon oil on the dresser. "Dust down all the wood, and you can head out to see your sister, 'cause I's gonna need ya back to help with supper."

# # #

"Hello?" Janie tiptoed into the silent house, its door wide open to welcome her. "Brea, are you home? I can't blame you for not wanting to deal with me. I just want you to know I'm having a hard time dealing with myself, too. So maybe we can just sit down and have a cup of tea together. Like when we were little girls. I need you..." she yelled out to the emptiness.

"She just left. Went straight out the door and to the car. She left the door wide open, too. Was in a hurry, I guess. Still not speaking to me, either. I must have really pissed her off this time." Dillon rolled into the room. "I'm glad she is getting out some. Being cooped up with me all this time has to be hard on the woman."

Janie listened. He seemed different. He seemed as though he was feeling better.

"Is she going to be gone long?" Janie felt a slight bit of discomfort, almost the feeling of betraying Brea by being alone in the home with Dillon.

"Don't have a clue. She never expects a thing from me, even after all the heartache I've given her. I believe she deserved a man that would change his ways — you know, become that person I was when I asked her to marry me."

Dillon rolled his wheelchair across the room. "Janie, you are the only one I ever was completely myself with. I've always had that fire burning, that yearning to see the world... Then, when your sister and I started seeing each other, she somehow cooled it, calmed it. She gave me a yearning for contentment. We were getting older; hell, the whole town was getting older, getting married, having babies. It was as if contentment was just what you did. So we did."

"I honestly came to make things right between me and my sister. Not to figure out the whys and hows of us, or the whys and hows of you and her. There is something I need for you to know. I'm just not ready to tell you yet."

"You know, part of me believes she thinks I married her 'cause it was the closest thing to having you. But it wasn't," Dillon interrupted. "The two of you were complete opposites. What made me fall in love with her was the opposite of what I loved about you. I guess you were what the boy in me needed, and she was what the man in me needed." He rolled the chair to the wall. "Hey, I wanna show you something." He stood, slowly, shaking slightly at the knees.

"Wow!" Janie said. "You'll be out of that chair before you know it."

"I can't tell ya how great I been feeling. Doctors said I'd never walk again. Paralyzed from the neck down. Hell, your sister had to feed me there for a while. She wouldn't leave my side. She even got me this chair when the doctor said I would be in bed for the rest of my life. And had the ramp built." He nudged his head toward the opened door. "They didn't think I was gonna make it. She had hope in me, more hope than I had in myself."

Janie knew that about Brea. Brea had always believed in her, too.

"Then one day, she stopped sitting by my bed, stopped saying my name. That was when she started sleeping a lot and doctors was sayin' she was depressed. So I laid there and knew I needed to get up so I could help her. Be there for her, you know?

"First feeling started with my chest. I started feeling my heart pounding. Then my fingers started getting feeling. After a day or two of trying, I was finally able to make my way to the wheelchair. Been taking care of myself since. Every day I am a bit stronger than the last."

Janie walked toward the mantel where all the family pictures were. She pulled the chain Marva had given her from her pocket and laid it next to the picture of Brea and herself as young girls. A coincidence, in the picture they both wore matching necklaces.

"Dillon, I have something I need to tell you." She stared at his and Brea's wedding picture and the photos of Dillon's and Brea's children. "We have a child together."

Silence filled the air and there was no hope of casual conversation coming back. "That is the reason I left. I was pregnant, too young to have a baby, and I wasn't ready to be held down with responsibility." Her back was still facing Dillion. "I put the baby up for adoption. I received a letter from an attorney that is representing him, and he wants to meet his family."

Chapter 11

"Well, my biggest regret is finally out," Janie grumbled as she jiggled the stick-shift into neutral then pulled the emergency brake up. She turned off the ignition. In her car on Ms. Francis' gravel driveway, she sat, just staring ahead at the gate to the back yard. As to why, she wasn't quite sure. The need to explore the secret was stronger now more than ever. Maybe because she'd just revealed her darkest secret, maybe what was behind that fence was someone else's dark secret — or fear.

"Hey." Thomas stood peeking into Janie's parked Datsun's passenger-side window. "You are back early. How did it go?" Tommy sat out on a quilted blanket spread across Ms. Francis' front lawn. Thomas watched Janie noticing how Tommy sat unconscious of the beautiful world surrounding him. "I thought he could use a good dose of some Florida sunshine. He needs to produce some vitamin D." Thomas smiled.

"Better than expected, I guess." Janie climbed out through the passenger-side door. "Still haven't gotten to work this out with my sister yet, but I took care of one of my skeletons." She propped her hands on her hips and turned toward Tommy, analyzing his obliviousness of Thomas' beautiful sentiment for his life. Probably the same unawareness her unborn child had thirty years ago about her own wishes for him. But she was well aware of what she had done. She'd slept for weeks after they had taken him from her. *Quit being so hard on yourself. He had a better life than I could have given him.*

"Where's Ms. Francis? I thought I could help her out some this afternoon. Get my mind off some things, you know?" Her eyebrows gathered from overthinking.

"I think she was working on Marva's room," Thomas said as he walked over to Tommy to rotate him, to give him another view of the lawn. Then he sat down on the quilt with his boy, picked up his guitar, and began to strum.

# # #

Janie stood, silent at first, in the doorway of Marva's room. She watched Ms. Francis cleaning the room, then she finally made herself known. "You need any help?"

"Oh, you is back. Did you get to see your sister?" Ms. Francis asked.

"No, but I did get to make things right with my brother-in-law, Dillon." Janie entered the room and scooped the dirty sheets from the floor. Ms. Francis' back faced Janie, and all movement stopped from her. Dead silence filled the room.

"Child... I believe it's time I tell you about my back yard." Her back remained facing Janie. "You see..."

"Finally! It has been driving me nuts," Janie interrupted, obviously making light of the backyard ordeal. She really could use some silly explanation of the stupid backyard secret. "I'm sorry I interrupted you, though. Please, go on," she added, realizing Ms. Francis was serious.

Ms. Francis turned to face Janie. No, she certainly did not seem to be taking it as lightly as Janie was. Janie straightened and began to listen, cradling the sheets in her arms.

"There is something sacred about that soil in my back yard. When I bought this place, there weren't no fence." Ms. Francis shook her head. "Just a story handed down from the town's old white folks, a supernatural legend.

I had to put that fence up to keep people out. People who had lost their loved ones. My house kept filling up with guests."

She turned to wipe down the dresser where Marva kept all her jewelry. She stopped again to explain, "They weren't just guests, which took me a while to figure out; they were the people's lost loved ones." She grabbed an unruly blanket from the top of a nearby chest of drawers, neatly folded it, and returned it to the chest's top. "They were burying the remains back there — mostly their ashes, but sometimes it would be something as simple as a lock of hair." She chuckled. "One woman even buried her husband's underwear, and sure enough he showed up, too." She solemnly added, "I's not sure why or how, but I knows God always has a reason for it. You see, I wouldn't be able to spend time with my little Annie if it wasn't for that soil. So God be takin' care of me, cause I's takin' care of the guests."

"Annie is one of the guests, too?" Janie asked, still holding the sheets in her arms.

"Drowned in the pond on the other side of the tracks. My poor baby wasn't ready to go. She had just started first grade. Her momma was home, passed out, when she drowned, and never knew Annie had left the house. I think she was on her way to see me," Ms. Francis softly said. "I found her. She must have been floating a while when I did..." Ms. Francis took a breath and continued. "Only thing I could think of doing was burying her in my back yard." Janie watched a tear roll down Ms. Francis' cheek. "Them guests, they always know when I's gonna get a newcomer. They'd told me a newcomer was coming, but I never thought it was gonna be my little Annie."

"So they know they are dead?" Janie asked.

"Sure they do. They's knowin' everything. I don't think they knows right away; it takes time for their souls to feel it. To feel the body release itself. Little Annie says it feels more like living than when she was alive. Like everything we know is magnified, sweeter than living, is how she explained. Much more life than the ones on the other side of the fence, the ones like us."

Janie shivered at the idea she had been living and communicating with ghosts. "I can't believe they are all ghosts." She just stared ahead.

"Guests, child. They's guests," Ms. Francis corrected. "I knows I keep sayin' we got to take care and make things right, which all these guests, they do's that, yet they still here. I don't know, child, but maybe it's the ones on the other side of that fence that's needin' to make things right. Probably why I don't go and try to get my daughter the help she needin'." Ms. Francis' lips flat lined. "I could lose my little Annie." After a moment of silence, Ms. Francis added, "You and me's different than them guests. We still got life running through us."

"I almost died in a car accident," Janie admitted but still contemplated the idea of every one of the guests being a ghost. "I still have some flashbacks of it, but I've also lost a lot of my memory."

As Janie stood in a paralyzed state, Ms. Francis grabbed the sheets from Janie's arms and threw them towards Marva's open door. "We just like them people on the other side of the fence, you know. Wanting our loved ones to keep close, but maybe we is wrong. Maybe we keeping them from going to see God." Ms. Francis stopped in front of Janie and made eye contact with her.

Ms. Francis clutched Janie's shoulders. "That's why your sister was here. She was burying ashes in my back yard," Ms. Francis finally admitted.

"What? Whose ashes?" Janie asked. "It *was* Brea..." She broke away and, simply deflated, stared down at the wooden floor.

A creak in the hardwood flooring just outside of Marva's room announced, "Her husband just passed away. That's whose ashes." And Marva entered the room.

"Dillon? No... I saw him, spoke to him. He was getting better, stronger." Janie's face drained of its color. "You are wrong — completely wrong. He is not dead. He can't be. I saw him!" she yelled then pulled herself together, knowing what Dillon had told her earlier about feeling better and how Brea had been acting. "Even if he was, how could I see him before his remains were buried in the back yard?" Janie paced the room, hysterical. "He can't be dead!"

"Like I say, child, it takes time for the soul to realize the body is gone."

"Nope, he is gone — so gone that she was carrying his ashes in her hands." Marva smirked. "He is the newcomer everyone's been expecting, Janie. Go ahead, take a look in the back yard now," Marva insisted while admiring her clean room with a swipe of her finger on her dresser. She must have been eavesdropping on the whole conversation.

"No! That back yard is off limits to Janie. And Ms. Marva, you needs to mind your own business and take care of what you needs to be making right," Ms. Francis instructed, glaring at Marva with eyebrows narrowed and hands perched on her hips. "Janie, we still gots life running through us, so we can make things right on this side of the fence. Ya hear me?" Ms. Francis pleaded with Janie.

"Oh Brea," Janie sighed, her knees ready to buckle. "I need to go..." She steeled herself and stared out the darkened windows of Marva's room. "I need to be there for her." Janie turned and ran out of the room, down the staircase, and through the screen door to her car.

Moments later, she pulled the Datsun into the paver-stone driveway, not remembering the trip over to Brea's home. She noticed the plywood ramp was no longer lining the porch steps. Janie crawled out of the car and stood. Brea's car was solemnly parked. The sadness she felt was so much stronger now than when she had arrived days ago. The door to the house once again stood ajar. "Oh dear... Marva was right."

# # #

Janie stood, silent in the doorway of Brea's home. The home Brea and Dillon had shared as man and wife. The home in which their children had been raised since birth. The home their grandchild would now occupy on occasion with cookies that grandma had made. The home Brea had become a widow in at the early age of fifty.

"I know why you are here. He is gone, dead, and who do I blame? You! So neither one of us can have him now," Janie heard coming from the living-room fireplace mantel, where Brea stood holding the necklace Janie had left earlier. "His last words to me were 'Live a little, Brea,'" she muttered. "Then he jumps in that sporty little car and speeds down the road. Imagine that — same last words you said to me," she said to her wedding picture. "You broke my heart, too, you know. And now you are back."

Brea laughed out with sarcasm. "Two broken hearts joined together in holy matrimony. Yes, you sure have come at a convenient time. And once again, you have made a mess of things, haven't ya?" Brea glared straight at their picture. "How about that life you so desperately wanted to live? How did that pan out for ya?" The good sister Brea suddenly turned a three-sixty and was facing Janie head on. She glared into Janie's eyes. "How would you feel if your husband quoted his first love's name to you... then you find out he is hanging onto life by a thread?" Brea growled. "I'm not ignoring you now, am I?" Her rage was apparent. "How dare you come to my home." She glared more at Janie. "He left me heartbroken, just like you did."

Still too stunned to speak, Janie felt her eyes fill with tears. Her feelings where hurt, but she knew they could not compare to what Brea must have been going through. "I'm here for you," were the only words that came out, a whisper in the wind. They were obviously transparent to Brea and seemed to mean nothing to her, but Janie said it again, this time clearer and louder: "I'm here for you." Then she added more softly, "I deserved that." Janie surrendered. "I'm not here to hurt you."

Brea commanded to the air, "There is more I need to say. And you, just you listen to me. You may as well be dead with him."

Guilt consumed Janie. She had spoken with Dillon, but now that she was certain he had passed, she finally understood what was happening. She needed to remind Brea of their gift. Something she thought she had outgrown. She'd always believed it was her imagination, but today she realized it was not. She and Brea had shared, as little girls, a secret something that neither one of them ever understood. They always referred to it as a secret power because that was what Grandma Chandler had told them to call it the day Momma and Daddy had buried her. That was the same summer Brea had found Daddy in the garage with a pistol in his mouth. Neither one of the girls really understood why they could still see Grandma Chandler if she had died.

Janie suddenly realized all the craziness about the back yard and Ms. Francis' guests was real and not some weird dream she was trying to wake from. And Brea should be able to talk with Dillon just as Janie had done earlier today. Or had she already tried?

She did bury Dillon's ashes in Ms. Francis' back yard.

"Please, Brea, you have to know he is still with you. He hears you." Janie knew she needed to tell Brea about her and Dillon's child because at some point he would find his way to Dillon's family and to her. This moment was not the time for Brea to learn of him. It was too soon. She would not be able to understand it right now or be able to accept it. "Dillon loved you so deeply. What he and I shared was merely a moment. You guys shared a lifetime. You have to know this." Janie opened her arms, moving toward her sister, but Brea sharply turned away.

"You should go," Brea softly said. "I need to think; I need to fix myself right now. You don't have a clue how I have had to live, doing for everyone, being here for everyone, and you — you are the only thing I was unable to live up to."

"I, I..." Janie stuttered.

Brea sharply interrupted. "You go! You go and *live*! While the rest of us stay here caged in our world. Go!"

Janie had no other choice but to walk out the door. *Brea needs time. More time. That's all*, Janie reassured herself.

Chapter 12

Janie turned the car into the gravel driveway at Ms. Francis' house. Only Ms. Francis stood on the porch, looking out as if she was expecting her arrival. Janie climbed out of her car.

"Child, you is back. Come on, now. I's got supper gettin' cold on the table," Ms. Francis hollered from the porch.

Janie made her way across the gravel, and movement behind the tall fence caught her attention once again. This time, a hint of fear passed through her thoughts. The curiosity no longer nagged at her.

"How did your visit with your sister go?" Ms. Francis asked, snapping Janie's attention from the back yard.

Janie's thin lips gave no answer. Her eyes closed with the thought of the words Brea had said to her as the memory still flashed in her mind. "Not good," was the only thing she could say.

As Janie joined Ms. Francis on the porch, she asked, "Where is everyone?"

"Waitin' on you, child. Hurry up, now. My smothered chicken's gettin' cold." Ms. Francis patted Janie on the back. Her hands were warm. Janie could feel the current of life Ms. Francis had running through her. "You needs to come eat. Ain't nobody able to go without eatin', and you needs to keep up your strength if you is gonna be runnin' back and forth to see your sister."

Janie followed Ms. Francis in through the screen door. The house was dim. They entered the dining room, and everyone else was already seated, waiting for Janie to arrive. Her seat sat waiting as well. The empty chair still sat with no one to fill it.

"We needs to say the blessing," Ms. Francis began. "Bless us, Lord Jesus, for the food we is about to receive. Let it nourish our body and heal us. In Jesus' name, I pray. Amen." Spoons began to fill dishes.

"He has arrived," Mr. Norman mumbled as he took another bite of mashed potatoes. Only moments passed before footsteps on the hardwood floor followed. The sound was coming from the back door. As the footsteps entered the room, all motion in the room stopped. Dillon stood in the doorway of the dining room.

"Well, come on in. We been expecting you," lighthearted Ms. Francis quipped as she continued to eat. Janie sat motionless. Dillon was there in the dining room of Ms. Francis' big yellow house. He looked fabulous. Tall, handsome, and healthy. He walked to the empty seat as if he had never been injured.

"Hello, Janie." He nodded and pulled the seat from the table. "I was looking forward to seeing you again." He sat, looking around the table at all of the guests. "I appreciate your hospitality." Janie still sat with no expression or thought. Everything she had learned today had all become her reality.

"Go ahead and eat, child." Ms. Francis patted Janie's arm to remind her she was still alive. "You and me will talk later." Concerned by stunned Janie, Ms. Francis whispered, "Just you and me — no guests."

# # #

Janie sat, sipping a cup of hot tea out on the porch of Ms. Francis' house. Evenings were feeling cooler, and a scent of autumn sat back in the distance. She had not said much to Dillon. What does one say to a ghost? *A guest,* she reminded herself. Even if she did speak with him, what good would it do? He was gone, dead, and he was obviously here to make something right for himself. Or he would have just moved on to be with God, as Ms. Francis had said. Maybe Ms. Francis was right in theory; maybe it was us, with life running through us, that needed to make things right on this side of the fence.

"You are just as beautiful today as you were the day I fell in love with you." Dillon stood beside her. "May I?" He motioned to the rocking chair that sat empty.

"Oh yes, sit," Janie nervously answered.

"Why am I here, Janie?" Dillon asked, staring out toward the railroad tracks. "And you are alive and well, yet I have been able to see you, communicate, and feel your life." His demeanor changed from curious to saddened. "I can't hear her any more, Janie. I can't see her. I can't even tell Brea I love her..." Sorrow filled the air.

"I'm not sure myself, Dillon," was all Janie could say. Moments passed as she took a sip of her tea. *Where is he trying to go with this?* "I was just sitting here wondering all of this myself."

"You need to tell her about our son," Dillon finally said.

"She isn't ready for that yet. She is a mess, Dillon. Finding out about him, right now, would destroy her." She turned to Dillon. "Not a day passes that I don't think of him. I regret my decision to give him up. But then I see how my life turned out over the years, and it really was the best thing for him

I could have done." She reached out to touch his arm. His cold arm, which now seemed transparent. *A guest*, she reminded herself. She was saddened by what she'd endured and how self-destructively she had lived.

"I wasn't the same person you knew, Dillon. Maybe my search for life outside of this place lead me to a type of death of *that* me. I don't know what I am saying, but what I do know... Maybe my idea of blaming this place for giving me heartache was wrong. Maybe it was protecting me." Janie paused. "I was just too busy trying to fight my way out to notice."

"She needs to know about him, Janie, and you need to be the one to tell her." Dillon peered into her eyes. "She can't find out any other way."

"I know," Janie agreed. "It just isn't time."

Silence filled the space as they sat staring into the evening, watching just as the dew began to coat the ground. Just enough to feel moisture. No more or no less.

The one thing that Janie noticed with all of the guests was a sense of contentment. Nothing of misery, with the exception of Marva, but even she seemed content being who she was. Maybe they were just here in this house, waiting for the outsiders to release them or make right whatever it was that needed to be right.

Dillon reached his hand to hold Janie's tense ones. To Janie, his touch was warm and inviting.

Unlike how she had felt when she had touched him. "I now understand why you are here, dear Janie." His brilliant smile erased her thoughts just as quickly as the day had turned into night. "We both need patience, just as my sweet Brea needs it." In the distance, Janie kept hearing Ms. Francis' words: "Child, they knows everything."

Janie smiled. "I guess I'll be staying here longer than I expected."

"Me, too," Dillon agreed. "But who better to be stuck with?" He stood from the rocking chair and leaned in, hovering over Janie's chair. It made her nervous. A slight fear of betraying Brea raced in front of her mind. This was not her. Not anymore. She had changed; none of this was about her.

Nevertheless, for a just an instant, it was she and Dillon fighting hormones and first-love heat. Primal lust with no concern of consequence. Terrifyingly familiar.

In that moment, Dillon kissed her on the forehead, a warm, soft connection. He eased her from the worry of making another bad decision. The kiss was nothing but a mutual love they shared — their love for Brea.

Dillon smiled. He knew what was happening, and Janie was determined to make things right for him, the son they shared, and Brea. Not once did she feel she was home to make things right for herself. And now she saw the mistake she had made thirty years ago.

# # #

Janie turned the knob to her room and entered with the determination of what needed to be done and what needed to be said to Brea, thanks to her talk with Dillon. She loved him, but now it was more of a connection of mutual love, not that teenage crush.

She slowly closed and locked the door behind her. Exhausted, she turned to face the layout of the room. Leaning against the locked door, she melted, sliding down to the wooden floor. Patience, all they needed was patience.

As the car slowly stalled, Janie glanced down and noticed her car had just run out of gas — directly on top of the railroad tracks. She snorted at the fact she needed to get out, push it across the tracks, and hike to the nearest gas station.

She started to push her door open and step out, but the sound of a train whistle pierced the air and she jerked her gaze upright. One bright light sped towards her. Within seconds, the train slammed into the Datsun. Black shadows and white flashes of light were all she knew as the rumbling and screeching of crushing metal screamed in the darkness.

Janie quickly woke to the pounding of her heart. She looked around the room and sat up in the four-post bed. The rumbling of the train shook the house. She was not imagining it. It was certainly happening. She quickly raced to the French doors, swung them open, and sure enough: the tracks outside of the house sat desolate, which eased her panic. What a nightmare she'd just had. To calm her thoughts, she grabbed for a smoke from a pack on the table. As she lit the end and drew in, she watched as the bugs of the night circled the outside light. A moth darted across the yard and made its way to the streetlight that shined upon the rusty tracks.

Why had she dreamed such a horrific nightmare? She stood, still panicked over what her dream had shown her. And why was she having these blackouts? She had awakened dressed in her pajamas and already in bed. What could be causing all of this lost time? The last thing she remembered was coming in from her talk with Dillon. Then everything after that she had no recollection of. The episodes were becoming more frequent, and each time it happened seemed to be after she had returned from seeing Brea.

A knock at her door startled her. She put her cigarette out in the ashtray and entered her room just as the second round of knocks sounded. Janie opened the door just a crack.

Ms. Francis' white eyes peeked in through the crack. "Child, you's feeling all right?" Concern floated from her as Janie opened the door further. "I heard screaming coming from here." Ms. Francis scanned the room.

"Oh, I just had a nightmare is all," Janie explained. "Ms. Francis?" Janie asked. "Can we talk? I mean, I'm going through such strange things — nightmares, and blackouts, and... I guess what I'm asking is..." Janie tried to get the nerve up. "Am I a guest, too?" Janie was always very imaginative, and well, ever since she had arrived, nothing was normal. Could she be a guest?

A smile spread across Ms. Francis' face. "Heavens no, child. I told ya, you and me has life running through us. Maybe you is just getting drained from all the running you been doing." Ms. Francis felt Janie's forehead. "You feel warm. Maybe you is comin' down with a sickness or something."

"Maybe," Janie blew out a sigh. "I just don't feel right. One minute, I'm fine. The next, I feel like I'm losing my mind." Janie rubbed her temples.

"Child, you needs to rest. You's not looking good — all pale, and you is shaky, too. And you ain't no guest, either. Now quit worrying and try to gets some rest." Ms. Francis backed her way from the room. The door closed.

Before Janie could even get back to her bed, there was another knock at the door. She turned and opened it again. "Child, you feeling all right?" Ms. Francis asked, concerned.

What was happening to her? Janie stood, stunned. Was she just reliving her whole conversation with Ms. Francis? "I heard screaming comin' from here." Ms. Francis scanned the room.

"Nightmare. Just need some rest, I guess..." Janie answered this time the best that she could.

"Okay, then you gets some rest. Can't have no sleepyhead helping me take care of these guests, ya hear?" Janie slowly closed the door, nodding as Ms. Francis faded into the darkened hall. What in the hell was happening? She needed to rest, she needed to pull herself together. She crawled into the bed with her heart pounding, head throbbing, and hands shivering. Maybe she was just coming down with something. Maybe all she had known since she had come into town was just one big nightmare. Janie slowly drifted off to sleep.

Sitting on a tree limb that leaned over top of the pond water, seventeen-year-old Janie and eighteen-year-old Dillon sat, swinging their feet enough that their toes skimmed the water.

"Well, Mr. Dillon, tomorrow I'll be eighteen and legal to do whatever I want," she whispered into his ear. She shot a smile to his reflection in the water.

Dillon smiled back at her reflection. Then he whispered in her ear, "Well, what do you want, Ms. Birthday Girl?"

Janie giggled, "For me to know and you to find out." She jumped from the limb into the shallow water. With a handful of water, she splashed at Dillon. "I want to live!" She spun in the water. "I want us to be together, too." She raised her eyebrows, looking for a response. "You know what I'm talking about?" She raised her eyebrows again, waiting for his answer.

Dillon jumped from the limb, splashing Janie's white top just enough that her bra's lace trim highlighted her plump breasts. He pulled her towards his tall, firm frame and laid a tender kiss to her lips.

"You and me, Janie." He dipped her back until the tips of her hair touched the water. "It's about damn time." He smiled.

Two soft knocks at her bedroom door awakened Janie. Could it be Ms. Francis again? She hadn't had another nightmare, so there was no way she had screamed out. Her dream... It was a wonderful dream. It was at the pond out on County Road 10, just like when they were teens. She threw the covers from her legs and was surprised to find her bed was wet where her feet had been. Confused, she made her way to the door and opened it slowly.

"Ms. Janie? Are you feeling okay?" Nelly softly asked, her hair completely pulled back tonight, and she was speaking full sentences to Janie. "You haven't come out in a while," Nelly added.

Janie was surprised Nelly was outside her door, and she wasn't quite sure why everyone was so concerned for her. Maybe it was the fact that Dillon had finally joined the group of guests. "They knows everything, child," Ms. Francis' words floated in with Janie's thought.

"Honey, I just need to rest," was all Janie could say at first then added, "but thank you for being concerned."

Nelly's thin lips' corners turned, and she gave a nod and gently walked away. Janie watched then slowly closed the door behind her. *I need to get some rest.* She returned to the bed, and the wet area had miraculously dried. She shook her head and crawled back under the covers. After moments of trying to clear her crazy thoughts, she gently floated back to sleep.

Chapter 13

Morning arrived as usual, just as the train's sound arrived reliably every night at three a.m. The sound of the train that had not run the track in ten years, although Janie continued to hear the train every night, the rumbles, the whistle, and the steps that followed. She remembered Ms. Francis' words as if they were set in stone, a stone Janie desperately needed to keep throwing at herself to keep out of harm's way. Could she be imagining that train? At this point, she believed anything was possible. Besides, she had been talking to and taking care of ghosts for a week now. Or had it been longer? Whatever was happening to her was obviously what needed to happen. She was going to stick to her plan. Before speaking to anyone in the house, Janie tiptoed out the front door.

To clear her thoughts, she decided to go for a ride around the town she had grown up in. Maybe somewhere out there, she could find the answers she was desperately wanting answered. She climbed in the car and slowly eased her way out of Ms. Francis' gravel driveway. As she backed the car onto the street, she looked out of the windshield at Ms. Francis' big yellow house.

It seemed so uninhabited, but of course it was well maintained. Not even one of the guests was able to be seen. Even Ada, who was always rocking out on the porch, was not there. And the cats that always lingered were unable to be seen. Odd, as if the house was the gateway to another world.

Prepared to accept anything that was thrown at her, Janie drove peacefully toward town. She merged onto its main road, first driving past the site of where the old Cramers' hotel once stood. Nothing but land with a real estate sign perched in the middle.

She approached the IGA, the only grocery store in town, and it was still owned by the same Harrison family. *Locally farmed produce* danced across the storefront window. Sure enough, old Mr. Jenkins was still alive and set up out front, selling his catch for the week. Janie was amazed at how different she felt compared to how much everything was the same. Sure, there were houses that had a fresh coat of paint or new additions added, but for the most part, there wasn't much to make the town unrecognizable, compared to how it was when she'd despised being in it as a teen. She embraced it for the first time in thirty years.

Down the sidewalk, a young girl walked, pushing a stroller in which a toddler waved a lollipop back and forth through the Florida air. The town moved slowly along as Janie proceeded to drive. At the only light in town, she rolled to a stop. There was no hustle and bustle of people. Just the easy, quaint story of what might have been. It had been her choice to leave; maybe she had done what was best for everyone else. In a weird way, she had convinced herself that she was being selfish. But her life had turned out better for everyone else. The heartache of her leaving was now her only regret.

She did a U-turn at the light and headed toward River Street. It was time to try to talk to Brea again. She took the back road along the tracks, avoiding passing Ms. Francis' big yellow house. She knew she would try talking herself out of going to Brea's if she did go the other way.

Within moments, she was turning into Brea's driveway. She noticed a pumpkin sitting on the porch. *Okay now,* she thought, *it is a little early to be decorating for Halloween.* On the partially opened door a flowered autumn wreath hung, and the smell of popcorn balls drifted to her as she approached the steps.

"Knock, knock," she yelled into the partially opened doorway.

"It's open," a much more chipper-sounding Brea responded. Janie noticed the furniture in the living room had been rearranged. The picture on the mantel seemed the same but with two new pictures of what Janie assumed was the new grandchild. "I went to see you the other day," came from the kitchen, followed by more of the sweet-popcorn scent. "They said you were resting, so I didn't stay long." Janie followed Brea's voice. "I spoke to Ms. Francis, too. Poor woman, still having to wait for that daughter of hers to get her act together." Brea stood at the counter, rolling balls of sticky popcorn and placing them on a tray.

How did Brea know where I was staying? Janie entered the kitchen. Had she had another blackout and not remembered telling Brea?

"Want to help? I get a ton of trick-or-treaters here, and I am known for my giant popcorn balls." Brea smiled as Janie stood, confused. Had time passed since she last saw her sister? Was Brea losing her mind? What was happening? Halloween already? Could Ms. Francis' house really be a place where time passed at the blink of an eye? "Wrap those while I get another tray going." Brea nodded her head toward the plastic wrap.

"I... I just came to tell you how wrong I was to leave you. This town..." Brea glanced at Janie for a moment then shot her a soft smile. "I mean, I was driving today through town and something made me realize it was myself I needed to escape and not this place. I regret leaving. Leaving you, Momma, and Daddy. I regret even leaving Dillon." Janie noticed Brea's eyes begin to fill with tears and her soft smile straightened, while not once did she look up. "Wait — let me finish." Janie held her hand up. "I believe now that my leaving helped all of you become closer. That is something I am thankful for." Moments of silence stood between them.

"Honestly, Janie, I never could leave." She dropped a popcorn ball on the tray. "I would love to have seen new places." She began to roll another. "You broke a lot of hearts. I felt I was left here to make everyone right again." Brea looked at Janie. "I'm not angry with you anymore. I know they say God has His reasons. I do see the gifts I was given, and what you had missed out on."

Brea began rolling another popcorn ball, obviously pondering what she might or might not say. "Do you know Momma and Daddy were both devastated that you left? Momma always blamed it on something she may have said or done when we were smaller. *That* I had to laugh at, because *I* didn't run off. And we were, like, always together growing up. She blamed herself, and Daddy — well, Daddy blamed Dillon for a long time." Brea stopped rolling and corrected Janie's technique with the plastic wrap. "When Momma was only hours away from passing, she made me promise to be here for you when you returned. Probably another reason I always stayed." Brea chuckled. "All she wanted was to let you know, no matter why you left, that we loved you, regardless. We did. Regardless."

Janie was speechless. What in the world was happening to her? Or was it Brea who had everything confused? Janie glanced out the window of the kitchen, and the Florida sunshine had a glow of autumn. Trees in the distance, too, held leaves of different colors. Could months have already passed by?

"There is something I need to tell you..." Janie began.

"There is no need." Brea raised her hand to stop Janie from speaking. "I already know."

Dear God, was Brea also a guest? Or another newcomer? *Child, they knows everything,* Janie heard Ms. Francis' voice in her mind. Brea wiped her hands on her apron and walked out of the kitchen.

Moments later, she returned holding Janie's briefcase. The briefcase that held the letter from the attorney. The attorney representing the adoption agency that Janie's and Dillon's son had contacted. Janie simply sagged.

"I contacted the lawyer, and I'm setting up a meeting," Brea added. "He wants to see you."

She knew. Brea had found out, and Janie was not able to give her the news. Janie just sat, stunned.

Could Ms. Francis have given Brea her briefcase? Could Dillon somehow have made it happen? Maybe she'd rested longer than she had thought.

"I don't know what's going on, Brea," Janie finally spoke. "I think I am losing my mind. How did you get my briefcase?" she asked.

"When I went to see you." Brea set the briefcase down on the counter in front of Janie. "I understand now why you left." Her beautiful smile was no longer there, only a face of understanding with a glimpse of a woman trying to accept the circumstance.

"Something strange is happening to me, Brea." Janie, exhausted, fell into the stool that waited for her at the edge of the counter.

"I understand you are confused, Janie. I am also trying to adjust to this. What I do know is we have to come together, just as we did as girls," Brea simply replied.

# # #

Janie drove, unconscious of her surroundings, down River Street. It was over. All of her dread of explaining, of making things right, all emerged overnight. She should be sighing in relief, yet she was not. Now she worried for herself, for her own mental state. Brea had taken control of their situation. Partly it annoyed Janie that Brea had all the say, but Janie admitted to herself that this was probably for the best. She was quite sure she was not very stable with her own thoughts. As for Dillon, he would be proud at how well Brea was handling this situation, and he should be.

As Janie crossed over the tracks, the memory of her dream returned. Maybe she was a guest at Ms. Francis' house, and maybe her dream was real. It would explain why she had heard the train every night. And why each day had come and gone as if she only existed as someone else, experiencing life through different eyes — eyes only she could see through. She gently shook all her thoughts away. *This is not happening...*

Within moments, Janie had arrived at the gravel driveway of the big yellow house. As always,

Ada sat on the porch with all of the lingering cats. In a flash, Janie noticed Dillon sitting on the porch with Ada, just as he had sat the night before with Janie, hunched over, smiling as he listened to Ada, with his forearms resting on his knees. *Being dead isn't so bad,* Janie thought. How ironic she had always claimed she wanted to live. Again she pushed the thought aside and climbed from the car.

Dillon shot her a quick wave from the porch.

"I'm back." Janie waved back as she crunched through the gravel to the porch and then stepped up onto it.

"This woman has had an amazing life," Dillon sat up and mentioned to Janie. "I can't believe how adventurous she was." He smiled with amazement.

"Wow, Ada, you'll have to tell me someday." Janie looked at Ada with a smile.

"Oh dear, sweetie, I don't think it is your time yet." Ada gently petted the calico cat that lay in her lap.

Janie held her smile long enough to not look perplexed at what Ada had said then turned to Dillon and asked, "Do you have a minute? I want to talk to you." She turned to Ada and said softly, "It's kind of private."

Ada rocked her chair. "Don't mind me. I already know." Ada smiled and winked at Janie.

Perplexed again, Janie just smiled. She felt a tinge of frustration that everyone knew things and she was in the constant battle of figuring out what the hell she was trapped in. A world of life or death.

She motioned for Dillon to follow her down the steps and into the yard, only to see him stop at the oak tree and not move any further. "Come on; let's walk the tracks like we did as kids," she said and motioned again.

"I can't," he replied with a grin. "This is as far as I can go." Dillon leaned on the oak tree. "We aren't like we used to be, Janie."

Janie stopped at the road and looked back, only to see the big yellow house was desolate and no one was around. Dillon no longer stood leaning by the oak tree.

Frightened, she took two steps back toward the house. There by the oak tree, Dillon stood smiling just as he had moments before.

Janie took two steps backwards toward the road and again the big yellow house was deserted. And no Dillon.

It is a different dimension, she thought. *How could Brea have come here?*

She quickly stepped toward the house until she could see Dillon again leaning on the oak. She rattled her head to remember what she wanted to say to him.

"Brea knows," was all she could say to start the conversation.

"I know," Dillon said. "She will take care of it. And you should let her. She is great with all that kind of legal stuff."

"He is my child!" Janie's voice rose then dropped to a soft mumble. "Our child," she corrected herself.

"You need to live, Janie. Aren't those your last words?" Dillon nonchalantly crouched and picked a blade of grass. He twirled it around his finger. "You need to figure it all out."

"That is not fair!" she yelled and pointed her finger at Dillon. "You can't throw that back at me!" She threw her hands in the air and turned her back to Dillon. "Figure out what? Figure out that leaving here was a mistake? Leaving you? Leaving Brea? Leaving my mother, my father? And getting some stranger to raise my child?" Janie crumbled to the grassy yard. "I did figure it out. I regret every bit." With her face cupped in her hands, she sobbed. "But I do know... All of you were better off without me here." She sank even further down, curling into a fetal position as she lay sobbing on the lawn.

Dillon pulled Janie from the ground, turning her to face him. "You need to pull yourself together now. You need to focus on *you*. That's why you are here." He stared her in the eyes. "Now is the time you need to focus on living, my Janie girl."

Janie girl. That was what Dillon had called her in their teens, his *Janie girl*. Dillon wiped the tears from Janie's cheeks with his thumbs as he cupped her face. Again, visions of their youth flashed before Janie's eyes. The primal feeling of youthful urges warmed her body. Life, more fiery than the rage her heart felt moments before. A pulling of the youthful girl she had been. The girl who wanted to live. Again, he kissed her forehead and all the desire faded, just as it had when she'd stepped in and out of Ms. Francis' front yard.

# # #

The aroma of supper floated up the staircase and into Janie's room. Panic struck Janie for a moment because she was not downstairs helping put together a meal with Ms. Francis. She hurried down the stairs and through the dining room where all of the guests were already seated, waiting on her to arrive. She stood as Ms. Francis balanced a platter of fried okra.

"Go on, child. Have a seat." Ms. Francis gently placed the platter onto the table.

"I'm sorry. I didn't realize how late it was." Janie pulled her chair back from the table and began to sit. "I would have helped you prepare supper."

"Child, it's all good. I knows you ain't been feeling all that well." Ms. Francis made her way to her seat. "You needs to get yourself well."

The table held fried cabbage, pork chops, lima beans and ham hocks, a casserole dish of peach cobbler, and of course the platter of fried okra. Everything looked inviting, and the scent made Janie's mouth begin to water. This was a good sign to Janie that her appetite had returned. Dillon sat a bit impatiently as if he, too, could not wait to dig in.

Ms. Francis began, "Our Father, bless us with this meal we are about to receive. Lord, we say thanks for having our time here together, in this home we share. Watch over each of us as we consume the meal of life. In Jesus' name, I pray. Amen." The serving of food rattled the table.

Janie was motionless, only feeling a bit strange at Ms. Francis' prayer. Today it seemed somewhat different, almost as if she was referring to her stay as something temporary. Janie supposed it was temporary for all of the guests and for herself. But something had struck her in an unusual way.

"You has gots to eat, child." Ms. Francis' eyes beamed at Janie as the older woman took in a mouthful of cabbage. Janie nodded and began to fill her own plate. Dillon passed the bowl of lima beans and ham hocks toward Janie as Thomas forked up a pork chop and slapped in onto Janie's plate.

Everyone at the table made sure Janie was being served. Janie again was struck; this was odd. She and Ms. Francis were the only ones who had been doing things for others, and today they were doing for her. Maybe she was a guest. Janie took in her first mouthful of lima beans. She scanned the table with her eyes. No one seemed to even notice how she appeared to be dismayed.

"This is de-lish," Janie spoke as she wiped her mouth with a napkin. And it was. The table of guests, including little Annie, just continued eating.

"I helped Ms. Francis change your sheets and get your room together this morning," Nelly quipped, breaking the silence. Her black hair was pulled completely back, showing her almond-shaped eyes and a thin-lipped smile that graced her face. Yet everyone still continued to not notice. They did not even notice that the guest that never talks was, today, talking.

Disturbed, Janie slammed her fork onto the table, "What is going on around here?" Janie's frustration was apparent. "Why is everyone so different?" she demanded as she abruptly stood. Everyone continued to not respond, as if Janie was no longer there. Janie could feel her blood pressure rise, and heat warmed her face. The room began to spin again, tunneling into darkness...

Young Brea stood above Janie as she lazily lay under the oak. "We could have a ladder and add a slide," Brea said as Janie visualized a tree house they planned to build together. "I could make curtains for the windows with pretty lace." Brea was always decorating and adding creative ways to enter or exit the tree house. Whereas Janie was more concerned with the concept of how she would make it happen.

"I could build the floor first with that plywood Daddy has behind the shed and use that old deck railing for the outside porch." Janie visualized this by framing the tree with her thumbs and pointer fingers. Brea and Janie were a team and always worked well together. They made things happen, until he blocked the vision.

"Hi, my name is Dillon." A silhouette blocked the sun and the girls' focus on the tree-house construction. *"I just moved in, two houses down."*

Brea was the first to say something to him. "Hi, we are going to build a tree house, right here in this oak tree."

"Me Tarzan-you Jane." Young Dillon snorted. *"We are, are we?"*

Janie sat up, annoyed by the interruption. She always remembered how her first impression of Dillon was not a good one. Boys were the enemy. At least at twelve. But by thirteen, she could not keep her eyes off him. Janie always blamed it on the summer sun changing her mind. And the fact that Dillon was tan and somehow grew muscles overnight. In one summer, he had transformed from a pale Northern boy that was skinny as a rail to a golden Southern dream. Janie and Brea also seemed to go through changes that summer. They both became young women less than a week apart, and their breasts had begun to protrude from their shirts. As for the tree house, it became a perfect teenage hideaway for the three of them.

White flashes of light made Janie feel paralyzed. The noise of beeping and humming machines surrounded her. "She is stable again." She heard the scraping of curtains sliding along a track, much like the sound of the scraping of metal as the train had made contact with the Datsun. The struggle to speak was real. Janie could not move. Paralyzed.

Janie, with every ounce of energy, forced herself to get up. She struggled. She strained. She visualized herself sitting up. With everything she had.

Janie finally sat up, swiftly noticing she was back in her bed at Ms. Francis' house. The sound of the train whistled in the distance. *What in the hell just happened?*

"She's awake." Dillon's voice came from the bathroom in Janie's room. "How ya feeling? You fell off your chair and whacked your head at dinner. Here — put this on that knot." Dillon pointed to Janie's forehead as he handed her a rag with ice wrapped in it.

"Ouch." Janie touched the egg-shaped knot that bulged from her head. "What did I hit?" She pressed the cold rag to the swollen protrusion.

Dillon chuckled, "The table, and it's in better shape than you are. What were you so angry about?" Dillon sat on the bedside next to Janie. "Ms. Francis said she was quite sure you would enjoy limas and ham hocks for dinner." He chuckled more. "She thinks you were angry because she didn't make the cornbread muffins."

Janie sat, quiet. She really did not know what in the hell to say. She was completely losing her grasp on what was real and what were dreams, visions, or her overanalyzing thoughts. "I honestly don't know. Everyone seemed different. I seem different." She hung her head. "Brea seemed different today, too. The weather seemed different. Everything is different." Janie looked at Dillon and whispered, "I think I am losing my mind."

Dillon reached out, stroked Janie's hair, and gently tucked a stray strand behind her ear. "You seem fine to me. You just need to get some rest." He leaned in and kissed her forehead.

"Ouch." She touched the spot where the kiss had landed right next to the egg-shaped bump. She reluctantly agreed. "I suppose you are right." With lips tightly sealed, the corners of her mouth slowly curled up.

"You know, there is a lot you don't know about Brea," Dillon said. "She wasn't always there for me like you think she was."

Janie sat, stunned that Dillon was opening up to her like this. "What do you mean by that?"

"She would have these episodes, I guess," Dillon began to explain.

"What do you mean *episodes*?" Janie pulled the rag from her forehead.

"A lot like how you were explaining your blackouts and how

it seemed like time had passed." Dillon stood from his seat on the bed. "She would just take off sometimes and would be gone for weeks at a time." Dillon paced the room.

"Brea?" Janie could not believe what she was hearing. This was nothing like Brea.

"Things got better about ten years ago. She left on one of her crazy adventures, and days later I got a phone call from a hospital in Memphis."

"Oh my God! What happened?" Janie asked.

"Probably the best thing that could have ever happened. She was different after that. She was back to being the Brea I had fallen in love with." Dillon stopped pacing. "I blamed you for her crazy behavior. It was like she was trying to be you." Dillon's left eyebrow rose as his lips tightened.

Moments passed as Janie relived in her head what Dillon had said to her. Then he patted her leg, "Go on and get some rest."

Chapter 14

"Janie? Can you hear me? Janie, it's Brea, your sister." Janie could hear Brea in the darkness. The struggle to open her eyes was taken over by her urge to follow the sound with sight. Her eyelids fluttered as she began to realize Brea stood over her. Janie reached to touch her forehead where the sharp pain of her head injury remained. At first, Janie thought Brea had come to visit her. Until she noticed she was in Brea's home, sitting on her couch.

"How did I get here?" Janie was perplexed.

"It's Thanksgiving. I made you some turkey and dressing. I also made Granny's peach-cobbler recipe," Brea said softly.

Janie was confused. Had she blacked out again? The last she could remember was dinner at Ms. Francis' with peach cobbler. She had become upset and then blacked out. Then Dillon had been nursing her knot on her forehead. "How long have I been here?" She rubbed her eyes.

"You got here about two hours ago. You looked exhausted when you arrived. Are you okay?" Brea asked. "You came straight in and plopped down on the couch. I just let you sleep. You looked like you needed to rest."

Janie regained a bit of energy as she sat up. "Brea, I know you know I am staying at Ms. Francis' yellow house on Moody Street by the railroad tracks. Strange things are happening there. There are these guests... that are dead," Janie started to explain. "Then there is the back yard. You know, the back yard where you buried Dillon's ashes?" Janie was in a rush to explain everything to Brea with hopes Brea understood why Janie was so frantic. "I have been a mess. I'm having blackouts. One minute I am here. Next I'm there. I wake up in bed. I have dreams of a train, and then I'm like paralyzed in a room of light. I don't know if I am one of them or just losing my mind." She went on for several moments, trying to remember every unusual incident. "Then Ms. Francis is very demanding that I stay away from her back yard."

Brea just sat, listening to every word Janie had said, but no reaction showed on her face. She seemed concerned for Janie and sat down beside her on the couch, but not once did she react to all the crazy nonsense Janie was telling her. Maybe Brea did understand what was happening to her. Brea let Janie finish and patted her on the leg.

With a sigh, she finally said, "Janie, you need to go to the back yard. I don't care what Ms. Francis tells you. The back yard has all your answers." Brea smiled, which Janie thought was odd. "Come on. Let's go be thankful and eat." Brea rose from the couch, pulling Janie's hand as she stood. "I even made Momma's broccoli casserole."

Moments later, Janie sat across the table from Brea, wondering if Brea, too, was one of them. She just watched and slowly took bites of her food.

"I have the meeting set up for the first week of December. I hope you can be there. He really wants to see you." Brea had finally spoken. "Oh, I want to show you something." Brea stood from the table, walked out of the kitchen into the living room, then returned holding a picture in a frame. It was a beautiful baby in blue.

"Oh, is that the new grandbaby?" Janie asked.

"It is. He sent me this picture a few days ago. It's your grandbaby, Janie." Brea just smiled down at the picture.

Janie saw in the picture the same beautiful eyes and nose of the baby the nurses had pulled from her hands the day she had signed the release papers for the adoption. A teardrop slid from her eyes as the salty taste of regret filled her throat. Janie absorbed his features until she was back at age twenty, holding her very own child.

"You need to sign right here." The attorney pointed to the line on the paper directly in front of Janie. Janie did not want to do it, but she knew she had no other choice. She had no future for this baby, and she could not return home and be a burden to her family. With the beautiful baby boy cradled in her left arm, she signed with her

right hand. Within seconds, the attorney snatched the papers and a nurse pulled the child from her arms. She watched as they handed the baby to the young couple that stood in the doorway.

Janie curled up in a fetal position and sobbed until she could no longer shed a tear.

"He looks like my boy did at that age," Brea said as she returned to her seat. "He has a lot of Dillon's features, don't you think?" She took a bite of her sweet-potato casserole. "I should pull out the photo album and go through some of the pictures with you." Brea continued eating while talking about her kids and about Janie missing them growing up. Just as she had with her own son. Janie knew Brea was not trying to be mean, but Janie could not help but envy her sister.

# # #

Flipping through the photo album, looking at Brea's and Dillon's children growing up and even at their wedding photo, Janie was sorry she had missed being a part of their lives through all those years. Seeing Brea almost explode with admiration as she looked at the pictures made Janie realize how close Brea and she had always been. Why had she run off from all of this? It was so comforting, and Janie had never felt anything even comparable to the feeling in all of her years away.

"Look at this." Brea pulled a loose photo from the album. "It's you and Dillon at the prom. My kids always thought this was us. I had to explain all the time that their father dated you first." Brea chuckled at the idea. "I have to say, it is going to be a lot harder explaining their new brother to them."

Janie did not realize how much of a mess she had put Brea into. Or how so many lives she alone had affected. By no means had she meant to cause her grief or heartache, but somehow it came with the territory. And Brea always took it in stride.

"Oh, wow! Look at this," Janie said as she lifted up a picture of their mother and father. Brea's glowing smile faded. "They are so young there. Momma's beehive hairdo... and Daddy looks like he is holding the world on his shoulders."

"That's the summer picnic. The day..." Brea's words solemnly drifted off.

"Gosh, I'm sorry Brea..." Janie quickly tucked the picture away. "I didn't realize." Janie looked up at Brea. She had never wanted to bring back that horrific memory, but she had. "Brea, you have to remember, if you hadn't found him, he would have gone through with it."

Brea huffed out a partial laugh. "Probably why I never left this place."

That was odd, Janie thought to herself. Dillon would not have lied about Brea's episodes, would he?

"Look — another one of you and Dillon." Brea pulled another picture from the album.

"Why did you keep all of these pictures of me and Dillon?" Janie asked as she scanned the picture.

Brea took the picture from Janie and stared down. "I like to look back at Dillon and you." She smiled, somewhat wistfully. "Makes me feel like I was a part of it, too."

# # #

Janie left Brea's home. Brea stood, sipping a cup of tea, in front of the big window in the Florida room. Looking out into her back yard, the old stand-alone garage sat at the edge of the property. Her garage of secrets, she called it. She had not been out there in years, until recently. She knew everything was different now that Dillon was gone. She had to make the choices of what was good for her family now. She needed to take control.

She always knew that someday Janie would return. Maybe a part of her always knew Dillon's death would bring Janie back, even if she only stayed for moments at a time. Brea needed her right now, and Janie needed Brea. Maybe someday she could explain to Janie why she knew everything about her life and how she really had gotten a hold of the briefcase, which held the adoption paperwork, but she did not want Janie to leave yet. She knew that secret would once again send Janie out into the world of the unknown. *I need her here with me, right now.*

On the glass table in the Florida room, next to the wicker sofa, sat Brea's bottle of anti-depressants. She glanced down at them and then decided she would take one. They helped, but once they wore off, her problems were still there, waiting to be noticed.

She was going to call Dr. Chang and arrange a meeting. Part of her knew Janie would object to the idea of Dr. Chang becoming involved, but it was probably best for Austin's sake. Austin was the child Janie had put up for adoption. Janie's and Dillon's child. Tears welled up in Brea's eyes, not for herself nor for Dillon and Janie but more for this child who was now a young man wanting to learn of his birth family.

Dr. Chang would probably cause problems between Janie and Brea, because Janie had no idea that Brea too had been to visit Dr. Chang. Although Dr. Chang was very open about Janie's visits with Brea, she never discussed Brea's sessions with Janie. They all needed the help from Dr. Chang. It was not just about Janie and Brea anymore. It was about Austin.

Chapter 15

Janie pulled the Datsun into the driveway of Ms. Francis' house. Had they noticed she was gone? Maybe they could explain what had happened to her during these so-called blackouts. Maybe all of what she had known of her entire life was something of a nightmare, although her time with Brea seemed like the only reality.

She climbed from the car and glanced to the backyard fence. Brea said to get to the back yard, but Ms. Francis objected to it. None of this made sense to Janie. Could the back yard really be some kind of sacred burial ground? And was she, too, buried there? Movement through the cracks of the fence pulled

Janie's attention closer to the fence gate. She reached out to open the gate.

"Not time." Ms. Francis startled Janie. "I needs help with supper." Ms. Francis seemed irritated. "Haven't seen you in a while. Where ya been?" It *was* her back yard. By no means did Janie want to invade anyone's property or privacy. But Brea had insisted Janie would find the answers there.

"Gosh, you scared me." Janie turned to see white-eyed Ms. Francis standing with her hands perched on her hips. "I'm not quite sure." Janie's head turned sharply back and forth at the fence gate. "I just... Brea said I would find my answers there. I... I'm not trying to defy you. I respect your wishes, Ms. Francis. But if my answers are there, then I must get back there." Janie moved closer to Ms. Francis. "Please. I need to know," Janie pleaded.

Ms. Francis looked at Janie, and as serious as she could be said, "If Brea says it's okay, then I suppose it will be okay." Ms. Francis smiled then lifted her finger. "But only after you earns your keep here."

Janie was suddenly relieved of all the pressure of her sanity. "That's a deal." She held her hand out to Ms. Francis. She was finally moving in a direction toward the answers she so desperately needed, even if it was not yet what she specifically wanted to know. Still, it was hopefully a chance to have answers to all of her questions.

"Come on, child. I gots biscuits needing cutting and my pot roast is needing some taters added to it." Ms. Francis' hand gently guided Janie's attention away from the fence gate. She seemed willing to let Janie back there, but Janie could not help but detect that Ms. Francis certainly did not want her there.

"Ada, I ain't got no more room up here in the big yellow house for no more cats, so you just quit feeding them strays," Ms. Francis said to Ada as they entered the house. Janie glanced over her shoulder to see more cats had joined Ada. Good news was Ada seemed as colorful as she once had been, just like her room.

\# \# \#

Janie balanced a platter of biscuits on a tray as she entered the dining room, noticing most of the guests were already seated — everyone but Marva, herself, and Ms. Francis.

"Child, we's gonna need some butter for them biscuits." Ms. Francis followed her words with a large roasting pan full of tender beef in savory juices. Potatoes, carrots, and celery circled the meat. "Oh, and grab that bowl of rice, too, when you come back."

Janie returned, holding a bowl of white rice in one hand and a dish of butter in the other. Ms. Francis was sitting along with the others when she set the items on the table. Yet Marva's seat was still empty right across from her and Dillon's spots at the table.

"Shouldn't we wait for Marva?" Janie asked. Everyone looked as if they had not noticed Marva was missing. She walked to Marva's chair and pulled it out to show that Marva was not there.

"That's your seat now, Janie," Dillon said with a strange smile on his face. He was right; they probably should keep some distance between each other.

"She finally not being so greedy and sharing some of her space. Now that woman was the last one I thought was gonna make things right, but she did. Go ahead an' sit in her seat, Janie." Ms. Francis nodded Janie into the seat. She began the prayer. "Thank you, Lord Jesus, for this nourishment of our bodies. And today, we wants to thank you for allowing Marva into your Kingdom. She may be a pain, Lord, but she got a good heart. In Jesus' name I pray. Amen."

Little Annie reached for a biscuit as Thomas patiently waited. Ada scooped up a spoonful of rice and plopped it onto her plate before passing it to Dillon. Mr. Norman drizzled the savory juice onto his plate and dipped a biscuit into the juice to soak as he patiently waited for the rice to make its way to him.

"She gave me matching necklaces," Janie interrupted the clattering of eating utensils. "Marva gave me two of her necklaces that matched. She said she always wanted a sister so they could wear matching necklaces."

"Marva?" Ms. Francis questioned, not really like she believed Janie.

"She insisted I give one to Brea."

"Hmm. Well, I'll be." Ms. Francis took a bite of her biscuit. Disbelief circled her expression.

Janie picked up her fork as she watched everyone eating just as they always did, as if the meal was their last. She took a bite. A chill ran through Janie's body. A cold, isolating chill. The motion of life around the table began to slow for everyone but her and Dillon. Something strange was happening. Only she and Dillon were moving. The others' motion froze. Time stood still. Janie's and Dillon's were the only movements at the table.

Janie scanned the table; her breath was warm as it hit the ice-cold air. A mist of smoky heat followed. She could see her breath. Dillon continued to eat as if nothing was changing around him. Janie took a bite, just observing the change in her environment.

The walls swirled, twisted, and folded as she and Dillon sat at Ms. Francis' dining-room table. All of the guests were still frozen in time. Dillon continued to eat. What was happening? The shifting of their surrounding rose-pattern wallpaper morphed into mocha-cream drywall trimmed in glossy pine. The whole dining room had transformed.

They were now sitting in Brea's and Dillon's dining room. Ms. Francis and the guests were no longer there. They were eating in the same room Brea and Janie had sat in earlier, looking at the photo album. Janie glanced out the window to see a red sports car in the driveway. Dillon continued to eat, not noticing the change.

Dillon then said, "You got to live a little, Brea."

Janie was stunned. Was she seeing a memory of Brea's? It was obvious, this was some sort of fight they must have had. Janie could not respond; something was holding her back. She felt in her heart that Brea wanted her to see this memory of what was happening.

"Sometimes I just wish Janie was back!" Dillon shouted angrily then slammed his fork down and stood, wiping his mouth on a napkin. He grabbed keys from the table and left, slamming the front door behind him. Janie watched from the window, the red sports car backed its way from the driveway.

Janie was saddened for Brea. That must have been the last time Brea and Dillon had been together before his accident. The coldness of the room surrounded Janie until she, too, was frozen in time.

# # #

Paralyzed again. A dark tunnel with light at the end. Only by sight, she floated her vision to the light. Bright lights surrounded her until a white room came into focus. Unable to move, she could only see and hear. Janie was nothing but thought. Janie tried to speak, but nothing came out. Her struggle seemed so real. Was she dreaming again? She was in a hospital room. Nurses were checking her pulse and the beeping machines that were above her head. Beeping, humming noises. Dillon entered the room. He looked ten years younger, as if she was having a memory, but this memory was not hers.

"Dillon." She tried to speak, but nothing came out. Her eyes, unable to blink, were drying in the cool hospital air. "Dillon!" So frantically, she tried again to speak. Nothing.

"Hey, my Janie girl," he whispered in her ear and kissed her forehead.

Janie struggled to show some way that she was there. But still nothing. A nurse entered the room and pulled Dillon aside. Janie strained to hear the conversation, but the buzzing, beeping, and humming of the machines masked the conversation.

Dillon returned to her bedside. He kissed Janie's lips and whispered again in her ear. "You are going to be fine, Brea. It is just going to take some time."

"It's Janie, Dillon!" she screamed but only in her mind.

At that very moment, a transparent Brea emerged from Janie's lifeless body. Just as Brea had done at their first encounter, Brea faced her paralyzed sister. "You may as well be dead with him." Janie struggled to move, each muscle in her body aching for movement. Again, nothing. Again, she fought to move with every ounce of energy...

Janie suddenly awakened in her room with her arms flailing about. What a nightmare she had been having. The train whistle in the distance sounded as if it was leaving town. Could that have ignited the nightmare? She heard the footsteps just like all the nights before, but they were coming from her bathroom.

Dillon emerged, wearing nothing but a towel. Janie glanced down at her body only to find she was lying naked in her bed. *Oh dear God, what have I done?*

"Janie girl... Brea. Whoever you are, I'm glad we are stuck here together." Dillon smiled.

"What the hell happened?"

"I started telling you how much I missed Brea, and next thing I know, you were her. I tried to stop it, Janie, really I did, but it wasn't you... It really was her."

Janie covered her breasts with the sheet. "Something is wrong here. I just dreamed I was her and she was me. It was a nightmare. She wanted me to be dead with you, and you called me Brea. I can't take this anymore. I need to call my therapist... I need to see her."

Dillon retrieved his clothes from the chair in the corner of the room. "I know you think all of this is some crazy dream, but maybe this is how your sister wanted it," Dillon said as he returned to the bathroom. "I am only a guest here," flowed out through the bathroom doorway.

"You are DEAD, Dillon!" Janie yelled, and then there was a knock at the door. Janie started to get up but realizing she still was still naked, grabbed her housecoat from the bedpost and put it on. Frustrated, on the final tie of the robe straps, she opened the door.

In the doorway, Ms. Francis stood and declared, "You can go to the back yard now, Janie," which floored Janie. "But you gots to promise me, child..." Ms. Francis' look saddened. "Promise me you's comin' back." With every crazy thing that was happening, could Janie actually think that the back yard was any different? By the look of Ms. Francis' face, the back yard seemed to be a threat to both of them. She thought about that along with her dream of Brea first violently screaming she wanted her dead and then urging her to go to the back yard. Janie was ready to scream, too.

Would the back yard really explain everything? Or would it just add to all the chaos? And now this problem she had just created with Dillon. It always did seem like Janie made a mess of things. *Probably would be best if I was dead,* she told herself.

A few moments passed after Ms. Francis had closed Janie's door, and only the sound of the shower running in the bathroom remained. Janie decided to tiptoe out the bedroom door and head to the back yard.

Barefoot, still in her robe, she stepped slowly down the staircase, hoping to not be heard by anyone. If she was going to the back yard, she was doing it all on her own — her terms, and no one else's.

She tiptoed through the house and into the kitchen at the back of the house then onto a small foyer porch. She hesitated, but looking through the screen door, it looked like a normal back yard. It was dark. It did not seem to be something she should be afraid of. She opened the door and stepped through. She stopped, instantly blinded by beautiful, bright lights.

Chapter 16

The bright lights flashed until Janie's eyes adjusted.

"Who are you?" Janie heard as her eyes began to focus. She was back in Dr. Chang's office. "What is your name?"

Janie was stunned for a moment. Had she blacked out again? Where was Brea?

"Janie Edwards," she finally answered the therapist.

"Do you know why you are here, Janie?" Dr. Chang asked.

"No, but I have a lot of things I want to ask you, Dr. Chang. I've gone to see my sister. I have been a mess. I'm having blackouts and nightmares, I'm seeing ghosts, and there is this black woman, Ms. Francis..."

Dr. Chang interrupted her, "I have your son, Austin, here, and he wants to meet you, Janie." She motioned for a young man in his early thirties to enter the room.

"Where is Brea?" Janie asked. *Brea needs to be with me at this meeting. Why isn't she here?*

Dr. Chang slid a chair in front of Janie as Austin approached. "Go ahead and sit," she said to him.

Dr. Chang pulled a chair up for herself and sat as well. "Brea arranged this meeting for you and Austin." She opened her notebook. "She thought it was best for both of you to meet under my supervision," Dr. Chang added as she peeked at them over her glasses.

Brea was right; it probably was best to have Dr. Chang here. But how in the hell did Brea know Dr. Chang? It still did not change the fact Janie was irritated that she wasn't informed, or maybe Brea had told her and it was during another blackout. She shook the thought away and looked at the beautiful man sitting in front of her. *This is my baby boy.*

"Hi, Austin," Janie said, just as she had said to him the day the nurse had placed him in her arms. He was a charming young man. It was apparent the adoptive parents had done a wonderful job raising him. She did not regret giving him up. *He would not have had such a great life with me,* she thought. Her only regret was missing out on seeing him become the man he was today.

Janie felt paralyzed, just as she had in her dreams. She was there — really there — but something had numbed her thoughts. Her sessions with Dr. Chang usually brought clarification. Today, that was not the case. Dr. Chang spoke of her to the young man as if Janie were not there, but she was. She felt even more confused about herself, almost as if Janie Edwards was some kind of secret person... or ghost.

Guest, child. They's guests, Ms. Francis' voice whispered in her mind.

# # #

"I met Austin. I met our child, Dillon," Janie softly said to Dillon at the table after breakfast had been served. All of the guests had gone about their daily routine of nothingness. "I don't know how I got back here." She cradled her head in her hands. "You have to tell me what is happening to me. And what the hell happened with us last night?"

"Nothing happened with us last night," Dillon simply said. Had Janie only dreamed that, too? "Now, three nights ago is a different story," Dillon added as he slid his plate away from himself.

"I blacked out for three days? I made it to the back yard. Then all of a sudden, I'm in my therapist's office. Then... today, I wake up in my bed." Janie sat, perplexed, still rubbing her temples. "That's all I can remember."

Could the back yard be a gateway to the physical world? Could the back yard be what is real and all of what was happening to Janie be only a part of her mind? That part that held the secret childhood place that belonged to Brea and her, their childhood super power? The more she thought, the more Janie began to think maybe she was a guest, maybe she had passed on and the car accident was where it had all happened. She did seem to have felt lost from that moment on, as if she had begun searching for something she couldn't explain and could not find.

"Janie, you need to know that we are all here in this house for a perfectly good reason. Brea has brought us here together. There was no mistake. She brought you here, just as she had brought me here," Dillon said, picking at his teeth with his pinky nail. "I know you don't understand, but eventually you will. I promise." Dillon smiled.

"I need to see Brea today." Janie wilted. No one seemed to be on her side. Or were they? "I have to find out what the hell is happening here." Janie was now convinced that she, too, was one of Ms. Francis' guests, but why would Ms. Francis always say, "We is not like them guests; we still gots life running through us," if Janie really was a guest? That moment, Janie decided she was leaving. Nonchalantly she rose from the table, not wanting to show she was going to leave. She casually picked up her and Dillon's plates. She reminded herself that she seemed to be the only guest who was capable of leaving. Maybe that was her thread of life that Ms. Francis kept referring to. She was going to the back yard again, determined to get the answers she needed.

She entered the kitchen and submerged the plates in the hot, soapy water before glancing at the entrance to the kitchen to make sure no one was watching. The foyer to the back porch was also clear, so she headed to the screened-in foyer. Just as it had the other night, the back yard through the screen looked pretty basic, like a common back yard. She opened the screen door and walked through, only to find herself standing in the front room of Ms. Francis' house. She had exited to the back yard only to enter through the front door. What the heck was going on? She turned around and went out through the front door this time. Ada sat on the porch in her usual spot, with all of the cats lounging around her in the shade.

Janie could see her car in the driveway. That must be her only way out. She would get in the car and leave to see Brea.

Janie made her way to her Datsun and climbed in through the passenger side. Once seated on the driver's side, she put the key in the ignition and turned it. Relief swept through her when the engine turned over.

"Thank God," she exhaled and began to back the car out of the driveway, looking over her shoulder and finding the movement of the car was not as fast as the driveway extending itself to the road. Panic struck her, and she slammed her foot on the gas only to hear the Datsun chug sluggishly, the gas gauge showing *empty*. The car slowly came to a stall. Her world, she realized, was no longer in her control. It was in control of her. It was confining her to one place.

She rattled the stick-shift to neutral. "Damn it!" she screamed. Frustration was as strong as the confusion. She grabbed the emergency brake to keep the car from drifting. The blackouts had transported her. Now she tried to leave but only to find herself back where she had started.

"The back yard," Janie mumbled as she climbed over the stick-shift and backed her way out of the passenger-side door. She crunched her way through the gravel and onto the porch. She quickly entered through the front door while the screen door slammed behind her. Through the dining room she went into the kitchen and onto the back-porch foyer. She took a deep breath and again pushed her way through the screen door and out to the back yard.

Chapter 17

Janie stood staring into Brea's home through the partially open front door. The back yard had lead her this time to Brea's home.

"Brea?" she yelled out, but Brea was not there. She strolled through the house, and not an ounce of life was in sight. On the table sat the photo albums still opened up just as when she and Brea had reminisced. She slid her hand over the top of the pile, noticing the prom picture of her and Dillon that Brea had kept. She picked it up, only to find it was not her in the pictures. Brea and Dillon stood together, beaming at the photographer.

Janie was confused. She remembered posing for that picture, but it was definitely Brea in it now. That moment of realization, the realization that maybe she never existed, hit her like a ton of bricks. She screamed out again, "Brea?"

She hurried into the living room to find the picture of her and Brea as young girls wearing their matching dresses. The picture was still there, but as she got closer, she noticed that only one child was in the picture. It was Brea. She then raised her hand to her neck, only to find she no longer had one of the matching necklaces on Marva had given them.

Frantic, Janie rushed out the front door of Brea's home... and entered Ms. Francis' house through the back door.

"What in the hell is happening to me?" she yelled.

Dillon entered the porch foyer. "Go to the back yard, Janie. Brea is there waiting on you." Dillon grinned. "She has the answers to all our problems." He proceeded to get closer to Janie. It was scaring her. He was forcing himself toward her. This all was not making any sense. She turned, forcing her way out the screen door once more. The brightness of twinkling lights encircled her. The sounds of harps played in the distance as the brightness of the lights warmed her skin. Light, lots of light...

Chapter 18

Piercingly bright lights. Then Janie's eyes began to focus on a figure sitting in front of her.

"Who are you?" Dr. Chang asked. "What is your name?" I hesitated. Why? I was not quite sure. Maybe she was testing to see who would answer. So I answered as if I didn't understand the question.

"My name?" I asked. Dr. Chang would always start our sessions like this, but something seemed odd today, seemed very redundant. I was not even sure if I knew who I was.

"Who am I speaking to?" Dr. Chang asked me again, so I decided to finally answer her. She opened her notebook and began to write in it.

"Brea," I answered.

"And Brea, is your sister here?" Dr. Chang asked.

"No. She is at Ms. Francis' house," I solemnly replied. As a tear ran down my cheek, I continued. "It breaks my heart to let her go." I looked up at doctor Chang. "She was finally able to meet her son. That's all she ever wanted. I know she never wanted to be living so confined. It was always my fault. All of it."

"So you are aware, Brea, that Janie was only a part of your psyche then?" Dr. Chang asked and waited for me to respond. "Brea?"

I did hesitate for a moment. "Yes, I am aware of my condition," I stated. "I suffer from multiple personalities — dissociative identity disorder — and Dillon's death brought on the appearance of Janie again."

"And how many children are swinging on the swing set today, Brea?" Dr. Chang asked.

"One. It's just me in the back yard," I replied.

"And in the tree house?"

"Just me."

"Brea, I know this is painful, but when did you realize you had a sister named Janie?" Dr. Chang asked as she scribbled more on the note pad.

"I manifested Janie in my mind" — I hesitated only to help clarify it to myself — "to cope with my father's attempt to kill himself. The summer I turned nine."

"Brea, who is responsible for putting Austin up for adoption?"

"Me... I am... Brea. I put my child up for adoption. My alternate personality, who I claimed to be my sister. Janie is who I believed had put the child up for adoption. I know now, Janie was only a personality I produced in my psyche. I was the mother of Austin."

"Good, good. We are making progress," Dr. Chang replied. "Where is Janie now?"

"She is gone. She's buried away," I said.

"You need to ground your emotions. Realize that you operate on a physical plane. It appears your emotions are stable for now. I am proud. Step back and evaluate what has happened. And give Brea the attention Brea deserves," Dr. Chang advised. "And your son, Austin is his name?"

"Yes," I replied.

"Are you going to continue a relationship with him?" Dr. Chang asked.

"I will."

"Who will continue the relationship, Brea or Janie?" Dr. Chang asked, concerned.

"Janie is buried. I, Brea, will have this relationship with Austin."

Dr. Chang smiled. "Very good. I hope we can continue our meetings on a regular basis again?" Dr. Chang stood from her chair and closed her tablet.

"Absolutely," I concurred.

"Let's do our imagination game." Dr. Chang paced around me.

"Where is Janie staying?" she asked.

"In the big yellow house," I answered her, just as Janie would have. "Off of Railroad Street."

"And what does the house represent to you, Brea?"

"The big yellow house is a figment of my imagination, part of my psyche," I answered only because if I went into detail, she would assume Janie was still here and not there with Dillon. Janie was always very good with detail. I smiled.

"And this Ms. Francis?"

"Ms. Francis is another form of you," I said. Knowing what question was next, this time I elaborated just enough, and with the right words: "Ms. Francis is in my imagination to help Janie, and you are here in the physical world to help me."

"Very good. And the other guests in Ms. Francis' house?" Dr. Chang asked.

"They are other personalities I have manifested over the years, but with your help and Ms. Francis' care, they are unable to leave yet still able to live." Again, I think of Janie and Dillon there together and how I can still have my time with him.

"And the back yard?" Dr. Chang interrupted my thoughts of Dillon.

"They are all buried in Ms. Francis' back yard..."

\# \# \#

After leaving the therapist's office, Brea returned home. She was going to do something she had planned to do many years earlier.

She went to the garage, her place of secrets and secret powers, and uncovered the blue Datsun. She did not know why she had ever kept that old thing. Brea got in, cranked it up. She pulled out of the garage and headed down River Street to Railroad Street. The Datsun pulled up to the tracks at the railroad crossing as the barrier arms began to drop. It was time for the train that passed daily. When she could see the train approaching in the distance, she rattled the stick-shift into neutral and proceeded to climb from the car.

At the back of the car, she pushed the Datsun onto the tracks, squeezing the small car between the two barrier arms until the Datsun straddled the tracks with the driver's side facing the oncoming train. The sound of the train whistle screamed louder and louder the closer it got to the Datsun. Brea turned away from the tracks and walked towards her home.

As the train made impact with the Datsun, the scraping and screeching of metal called for her to turn around and watch. Brea could see flashes of nine-year-old Janie on the other side of the tracks as the boxcars passed. Janie just stood, staring as the train passed...

\# \# \#

Austin stood in the doorway. He looked to be in his early thirties. A handsome man he was. He looked a lot like Dillon, but Janie's spirited eyes stared back at me. He did look a lot like my boy.

"Come in, please."

"I wasn't sure you were going to respond to my letter. I wanted to thank you again for our visit," Austin said and nodded. "I have to say, my life has made so much more sense to me now. I have also begun to have sessions with a therapist. I know they say it isn't hereditary, but I can't help but be relieved that my birth mother suffers from this, too."

"Oh honey, it isn't suffering. I wouldn't have myself any other way." Brea smirked. "It has its advantages. It is all in how you handle it." She gently patted Austin's back. "Come, sit..."

# # #

Darkness.

Janie tried to sit up, but something had her confined. It was dark, rich soil. She moved back and forth and could feel the damp earth loosen with her movements. She continued to move and was able to pull herself slowly from the ground. Where was she?

It was dark, but she could see the old eight-foot fence surrounding the space. The same fence that surrounded Ms. Francis' back yard. Janie looked down to notice she wore a blue gown a lot like the one she had worn in the hospital when she'd had her accident. She could feel the pounding of her heart, life running through to her fingers. Her legs began to fill with a tickling of life. Sweeter than life itself. She knew she had moved on. She knew exactly everything that had happened — why and how. She was Brea, and Janie was just another form of herself. Brea only held the physical form. She knew she was now one of the guests.

As she walked barefoot, she stepped around the other mounds of dirt, each marked by a stone with a name painted on top. Ada, Mr. Norman, Marva, Nelly, little Annie, Thomas, Tommy, and names of others she did not recognize. Right next to her burial spot sat a stone with Dillon's name written on it. His stone seemed slightly different from the rest of the stones. Her sister, Brea, must have buried both of their remains in Ms. Francis' back yard. She wiped the dirt from a stone that sat right in the middle of both of their adjacent burial plots. She was surprised what she read:

My Husband

and

My Dearest Sister

May you live the life I was

unable to give you

Mother and Father

of

Austin

Janie made her way into the house, the air inside silent, dim, and welcoming. She was now a guest.

Ms. Francis' voice echoed as Janie strolled through the big yellow house, "There is something sacred about that soil in my back yard. When I bought this place, there weren't no fence. Just a story handed down from the town's old white folks, a supernatural legend. I had to put that fence up to keep people out. People who had lost their loved ones. My house kept filling up with guests. They weren't just guests, which took me a while to figure out; they were the people's lost loved ones." The whispering voice of Ms. Francis followed Janie through the kitchen and into the dining room. "I's not sure why or how, but I knows God always has a reason for it. You sees, I wouldn't be able to spend time with my little Annie if it wasn't for that soil. So God be takin' care of me, 'cause I's takin' care of these guests."

Dillon sat at the table, smiling up at Janie. One flickering, long-stem candle sat in the middle. Only two settings had been placed at the table: one for her and one for Dillon. She now knew why she was there.

NOTE FROM THE AUTHOR

Being the youngest of four, I could never imagine myself without my siblings. My brother is a lot like my father, to whom no man could ever measure up in my eyes as a young girl. They just do not make them like that anymore. I cannot deny that I am married to one heck of a great guy, too. I have two wonderful boys, as well, but the relationships I share with my sisters are something that can never be severed.

I came up with this idea of *Sisterly* by the grace of God blessing me with two sisters who I admire, each for her own unique reason and personality. Sure, we have our moments of disagreements, but I share a sameness of some sort with both of them in the entirety. Before my mother in law passed away, I watched her two sisters care for her in her final days. The care and closeness I watched between them made me see and appreciate the importance of my own sisters.

Although this story is a story of its own, it brought out something in me that I honestly cannot imagine not having — gratefulness for the important bond my sisters and I share. You know how as we grow, we may say or do something that reminds us of being like our mother? That is also true for me with my sisters, possibly because I was the youngest sibling. I am a blend of both of my sisters. A mixture of some of their good qualities as well as some of their stubborn qualities. Without my sisters, I would have never become the person I am today.

In this fictional story, *Sisterly*, I was able to get that same metaphorical idea into words. As I said before, this story took on a life of its own. And I hope it will continue to live on for you just as it has for me — with a greater appreciation of my SISTERS. I love you both.

Photo by Janelle Barbour

ABOUT THE AUTHOR

Jorja DuPont Oliva, author of the Chasing Butterflies Series, has created another realm in her writing quest. *Sisterly* is her first psychological thriller, with twists and turns like nothing you have read before. A unique plot that will have you addictively turning the pages.

Photo by Trudy Tedder

ORDERING INFO

Jorja DuPont Oliva

P.O. Box 1774

Bunnell, FL 32110

Available on Amazon.com

WORKS FROM THE AUTHOR

Chasing Butterflies in the Magical Garden- Book One 2013

Chasing Butterflies in the Mystical Forest- Book Two 2014

Chasing Butterflies in the Unseen Universe- Book Three 2015

A Night Like This- Contributing Author 2016

Creative Chaos- Contributing Author 2017

Sisterly- first Psychological Thriller 2017

WORKS IN PROGRESS

Chasing Butterflies Screen Play

Cook Book

Poetry Book

WWW.jorjao2013.com

jorjao@msn.com

Bonus Material

Wait! Unusual happenings in this story…

I began this story with the idea of sisterly love. How sisterly love can conquer anything. As I finished my first draft, I had an idea of what each of my characters looked like in my mind.

First was Ms. Francis, a strong, God-loving caregiver who could cook. I ran across women like her in real life and in my hometown. Cilla and Annie really started out as part of my inspiration for Ms. Francis.

But let me step back a minute. When I was a young girl, my mother told me a story about a black woman she worked with at one of our local restaurants who inspired her. My mother grew up in the same town in which she raised me and where I am raising my own children. One day while my mother was at work, the woman — who by the way was a cook while my mother was a server — was running late, and the restaurant was in a frantic state. Since this woman was always on time and dedicated to her work, it seemed odd to all who worked at the restaurant for her to be late. She finally showed up, rushing in through the back door, ready to work, not long after the restaurant was ready to open. She put on her apron and began her job. Grant you, this was a time in our small town when segregation was still in effect. The black woman apologized for being late because she had birthed a baby that morning. At the time, my mother was just out of high school and beginning the first stages of adult life. This woman, with her strength and resilience, had inspired my mother enough to carry on that same story to me. Therefore, in a way, fifty years later, that same black woman is still inspiring me. Wait… Let me explain.

Cilla and Annie, the black women I mentioned earlier as inspiring my Ms. Francis' character, well, this is where their story gets to be a bit on the unusual side. The baby who was born in my mother's story was Ms. Annie. And…it gets even crazier. Her mother's nickname was "Sister." Ms. Francis has what I call the essence of the black woman I so much admired as a little girl, and today that admiration still holds true with Ms. Cilla and Ms. Annie. This was a meaningful coincidence, because I had chosen to write *Sisterly* long before Hilda Mae Hall, "Sister," had passed. I honestly did not even see the connection until I was in the editing stages of *Sisterly*. God always has a way of putting stories and people in your path to inspire you. After the passing of "Sister" was when little Annie was born in my story. Once again, that baby girl the inspiring black woman birthed, in the story told to me thirty years ago, now had a name to me. Annie Hizine. And I, too, work with her at a local restaurant — The Bantam Chef. Coincidence? I say it is fate.

These are inspiring black women. What grabs at my heart the most is- I was, just as my mother was, inspired by these women. Their resilience, strength, God-loving nature, and their cooking. So to all you black women and women in general, never take yourself for granted, because you never know who you might inspire.

As another odd coincidence, the diner I mentioned in my mom's story, then called The Bunnell Restaurant, today is known as The State Street Diner. My writers' group and I meet once a week at the exact location where my mother's story took place. This is where we meet to discuss our works in progress. So I guess in a turn of events, *Sisterly* was born in the same location. Neat, wouldn't you say? I have always loved how every connection made is as if somehow these stories are meant to be told.

More Bonus Material

You know, every time I sit down to start creative writing, mostly fictional work, a reality of some sort peeks its head out to show me it is still there. I love metaphors and looking at life through other eyes, as if I am seeing something for the first time when maybe it was there all along. When I began *Sisterly,*, I needed a character who had lived through many struggles and hardships. So I began to create her. Janie began to take life as I typed away on my keyboard. *Sisterly* was in motion, and I was creating the story I had been planning for months. I was living through Janie's eyes. And I was starting to see a lot of my own life regrets. No, that regret is not in this story. I try not to dwell on spilt milk and instead move forward to become a better person each new day. However, after the story was in the editing stage, I recognized Janie in someone who is pretty amazing. Jennifer Raymond.

It wasn't that Jenn was a woman who had naturally started out on the right foot and grew from there. She was a woman who in her younger adult life had fought battles she wasn't so proud of and which lead her to missing her children's younger years. Although heartbreaking to see her regrets, her effort is real, and I watch daily as she fights to make up that lost time with her children that she can never get back. I am overwhelmingly proud of her and hope she too does not dwell on her past, because today is the opportunity to be the mother she always was.

While I was in the formatting stage of *Sisterly*, another struggle landed in her lap: the loss of her father. Rest peacefully, Paul Bell. He raised her from a young age on his own, after the passing of her mother. A coincidence, Paul was going to be one of my models for the Thomas character, who also was raising his son. Unfortunately, his passing made me decide to go a different route with my back cover.

Life always has reasons for why things are the way they are. We aren't the ones in control of our final story, but as the chapters move along, we can always make the best with what we have. I always believe my finished book is what it is meant to be, regardless to how I originally wanted it or had it planned. A lot like life, it is the journey that is important and not the destination. I still want to share some pictures of what my mind pictured some of my "guests" looking like and of Janie's car…

"Ms. Francis"

Annie Hizine

J.D Oliva

"Thomas"

Paul Bell

Sisterly

"Little Annie"

Jerrricha Williams

"Marva"

Donna Ganert

"Nelly"

Mae Ann Bertolano Rozzelle

"Ada"

Linda DuPont

"Janie's Car"

Datsun 210

Jennifer Raymond and Paul Bell

"I've been at a loss for words for weeks, there just wasn't any way to explain what I was feeling. Even now to put into words it is hard, but today I celebrate the life of my father. A man who was everything to me. He was my best friend, my confidant, and my hero. My dad wasn't always an easy man. He was stubborn and hardheaded. He was hard working, he loved, and he always had the best of intentions. We were a lot alike, and it led to us bumping heads often. We went through our phases of not speaking and our phases where we were inseparable. Growing up, it was me and him against the world. We were a team; we tore each other down and built each other up over and over again. It is what we did. He was the one person I didn't have to lie to or pretend with. I could be exactly who I was, with every flaw, and not worry about not being accepted or loved as that imperfect person. He was who I went to when I couldn't be strong. He knew just what to say to make me laugh. We had this joke about a stupid carrot: all he had to say was "hippity hop," and it would make me smile. All I can say is that I wasn't ready. I wasn't ready to say goodbye. I guess we never really are. I just thought I had more time, but again we always think there is going to be a tomorrow." –Jennifer Raymond

Sisterly

JORJA DUPONT OLIVA

Chasing Butterflies

In The
Magical Garden

JORJA DUPONT OLIVA

Chasing
Butterflies
IN THE MYSTICAL FOREST

JORJA DUPONT OLIVA

Chasing Butterflies

IN THE UNSEEN UNIVERSE

Sisterly

A Night Like This

A Flagler County Anthology

CREATIVE CHAOS

JORIA OLIVA

MO H. RAY KING   T. G. AGIN

ROBIN H. SOPRANO   MEL JOHNSON

Sisterly

A Sister is someone to dream, cry, sing, laugh with

Made in the USA
Columbia, SC
11 December 2020